FROM THE
NANCY DREW FILES

THE CASE: While folding flyers for a political candidate, Nancy runs across a million-dollar mystery.

CONTACT: Nancy agrees to help a man who's broken the law—to trap a robber baron.

SUSPECTS: Michael Mulraney—the handsome builder has a shady past and a dark future.

> *Franklin Turner—the young political aide is rich, well connected, and very nasty.*

> *Tim Terry—the candidate for city council has plenty of charisma, but he needs financing.*

COMPLICATIONS: A mysterious kingpin is trying to gain control of millions in city funds—and he doesn't care how he does it.

Books in THE NANCY DREW FILES® Series

Available from ARCHWAY paperbacks

THE NANCY DREW FILES CASE · 33

DANGER IN DISGUISE

Carolyn Keene

AN ARCHWAY PAPERBACK
Published by POCKET BOOKS
New York   London   Toronto   Sydney   Tokyo

AN ARCHWAY PAPERBACK *Original*

An Archway Paperback published by
POCKET BOOKS, a division of Simon & Schuster Inc.
1230 Avenue of the Americas, New York, NY 10020

ISBN: 0-671-64700-8

First Archway Paperback printing March 1989

10 9 8 7 6 5 4 3 2 1

Printed in the U.S.A.

IL 7+

DANGER
IN DISGUISE

Chapter

One

I'LL BE FOLDING FLYERS in my dreams to-night," George Fayne said, running her fingers through her short dark curls. She stretched to ease the kinks brought on by bending over a desk.

"Just remember you got us into this," said Nancy Drew with a grin that made her blue eyes sparkle. "Being a public-spirited citizen can be hard work."

George grinned back. She'd been doing volunteer work on Councilman Tim Terry's reelection campaign for the last couple of months. Occasionally her friends helped her out. That night they were using the councilman's office to organize a voter-registration drive.

"Well, this is the last of these," Nancy said, relieved. She tossed back her shoulder-length red-blond hair and stuffed the last flyer into the last envelope.

"Bess was smart to opt for the store distribution detail. Folding and stuffing isn't very inspiring." George pulled a denim jacket on over her blue button-down shirt.

"I have a feeling she had her strategy planned from the start," Nancy replied. She remembered how her friend Bess Marvin had grabbed the first batch of flyers from the copy machine. She had said she'd take them around to the shops in the neighborhood—including the video arcade where Jeff Matthews, her latest crush, sometimes hung out. That was Bess's idea of public-spirited volunteer work.

"I have to lock up, then we'll go find her," said George.

Nancy picked up the Emerson College varsity jacket her boyfriend, Ned Nickerson, had given her. Although it was early September and the days were still warm, the nights could get cool.

George piled envelopes into a shopping bag for mailing. "This really is a good cause," she said, "especially if people register and then vote for Tim Terry."

"You're really in the councilman's corner, aren't you?"

"He's a great guy and a decent politician. I'm not the only one who thinks so. He has some very influential people supporting him. He's even got big guns like Bradford Williams looking at him."

"That is impressive, all right." Nancy had often heard her father, attorney Carson Drew, talk about Williams. The Chicago businessman had become quite powerful in the past few years.

"It's important too. It takes more than stuffing envelopes to run a political campaign. With the right financial backing Tim Terry can go straight to the top."

"Where exactly is that?" Nancy looked quizzically at her friend.

George pondered for a moment. "After this reelection, I'm not quite sure," she said, "but he's on his way."

"And we should be on our way too." Nancy slipped into the varsity jacket. "I'll go turn off the copy machine while you finish up here."

Nancy was surprised to hear voices as she walked down the dimly lit hallway. She'd thought she and George were the only ones in the office— the last of the staff had left an hour earlier.

The voices grew louder as Nancy got closer to the copy room. She made out two men talking. One spoke in an unusually deep bass, and he sounded very angry.

"How could you have done something so stupid?" he rumbled in the first words Nancy could hear clearly.

Nancy ducked out of the hallway into a shadowed recess, so that she was near the copy room door but not visible through it. She'd made the move almost without thinking—something told her the two men inside might not appreciate any interruptions. She peeked around the edge of the niche at the frosted glass panel of the door, but all she could see were blurred shapes. Quickly a second voice piped up.

"You made me nervous. All those threats on the phone—I rushed in here and out again and didn't think to check the basket of the machine. I must have left one of the copies in it by mistake." The second voice sounded pinched and shaky.

"You weren't supposed to copy them in the first place. You were supposed to turn the originals over to me and disappear." Nancy heard scuffling and then a squeal. "You were trying to pull a fast one, weren't you?"

"Let go of me!" The voice was choked as well as sounding nervous now, as if someone had the man by the throat.

"Oh, I'm so sorry." The rumbling bass words dripped with sarcasm. "Did I mess up your fancy suit? I guess I was thinking about how you might have gotten away with it—if I hadn't searched your briefcase and found those extra copies."

"I—I thought I needed them for protection." Squeaky wasn't choking now. The other guy must have let him go.

"The kind of protection you need, buddy, is from yourself. First, you try to double-cross me. Then you lose track of one of your copies," said Deep Voice. "Then we come here, and the copy

4

isn't where you said it would be. Check the count one more time to be sure."

Nancy heard papers being riffled.

"There're only five here. I made six copies. I'm positive about that, and this is the only place I could have left the other one."

Suddenly the smaller of the two blurred forms came into sharp focus as Deep Voice pressed Squeaky up against the door. Nancy could see black hair and a gray sports jacket, and as Squeaky tried to wriggle away from his captor, she caught a glimpse of his hawk-nosed profile.

"Are you sure there were only six? You'd better not lie to me," the bass voice threatened.

"I swear I'm not lying!"

Nancy heard a sharp intake of breath. She could almost see the speaker being strangled. She peered around her in the gloom, looking for something she could use as a weapon. Poor Squeaky might need rescuing, but she didn't dare barge in unarmed.

"Why should I believe you?" Deep Voice was saying. "You made those copies after I told you I wanted those papers so I could get rid of them."

"But I admitted I'd done it."

"Not until I slapped it out of you."

"And I don't want you to slap me around anymore. I'm telling you the truth. There were only six copies."

That response was close to sobbing. Nancy tensed for action. She couldn't let this go on.

5

"I believe you, buddy. You're too scared to lie." The bigger man gave a sneering chuckle. "So what happened to number six?"

"Somebody must have taken it out of the copier basket by mistake."

"Or on purpose. Maybe somebody else besides me found out you'd been poking your nose in where it didn't belong. Maybe somebody else got more curious than it's healthy to be."

"No, I'm sure that didn't happen," came the hasty reply. "Nobody but me would have understood the significance of that printout. There'd be no reason for anyone to take it on purpose."

"I'll have to check that out for myself. I don't like loose ends."

"What are you going to do?"

"Somebody who works here must have taken that last copy. So I'm going to search the offices to see if I can find it or figure out who was here last."

Nancy slipped out of the recess. If he searched the offices, he'd find George. Nancy couldn't let that happen.

She hurried down the hall and around the corner, moving quietly along the wall and keeping low. Every nerve was taut in dread of hearing that deep voice boom out after her.

Easing open the office door, Nancy slipped inside and crooked a finger at George. "Come with me," she whispered urgently. "Don't ask any questions. Just hurry!"

George didn't argue. She followed without a word as Nancy darted out of the office and through a fire door into the back stairwell.

Nancy motioned for George to get behind her, then flipped off the light switch and eased the door back open a crack.

They'd made it to their hiding place with only a moment to spare. Nancy heard footsteps enter the office she and George had just left. The fire door had squeaked on its hinges when they had opened it. If she opened it wide enough to see, the man with the deep voice might hear it. She had to content herself with listening at the crack.

She and George hadn't picked up anything but their purses or turned out the lights behind them. The men would probably conclude that whoever had been using that office was the last to leave the building and had done so in a hurry. Nancy had no doubt Deep Voice would find that suspicious. Still, he'd have no way of knowing it was George and Nancy, since they were volunteer workers, not regular staff.

"What's happening?" George murmured just audibly.

Nancy raised a forefinger to her lips and pressed her ear closer to the narrow opening. A long moment lapsed before she silently eased the door shut and slumped back against the wall.

"What's happening?" George whispered again, close to Nancy's ear.

"They were talking about someone named Kathy Novello. Who is she?"

"She's a secretary—that's her office we were working in. What did they say about her?"

Nancy straightened up and answered in a tone that she forced to remain calm.

"One of them ordered the other to get rid of her."

Chapter

Two

"WHAT?" GEORGE GASPED.

"Can you find her phone number? We have to get in touch with her right away," Nancy said grimly.

George searched hastily through the file, looking for Kathy Novello's card. Nancy filled her in on what had happened in the copy room, finishing up as she punched the phone buttons for Kathy's number.

"I've got her answering machine," said Nancy after a short wait. "She's not at home. We have to go to her place."

"She may actually be there right now," said George. "She lets the machine take messages even when she's home."

"Hello, Kathy Novello, are you there?" Nancy

9

said to the recording. Then she covered the receiver to ask George, "Why would she do that?"

"She always screens her calls. You know, in case she doesn't want to talk."

"Kathy, if you're there, please pick up the phone. This is urgent!"

"She won't necessarily hear you either," said George. "She turns down the volume, too, so she may not even know there's a call coming in. She says she hears more than enough jangling phones here in the office."

Nancy flashed an exasperated look at George. "Kathy, this is a friend calling. You are in danger. Please listen—get out of your house immediately."

"You have to meet Kathy to understand," said George. "She really keeps to herself. Sometimes she just turns the phone off for privacy."

Nancy slammed the receiver down and headed for the door. "Well, this time it could turn out to be the biggest mistake she's ever made."

George snatched the file card with Kathy's address on it and hurried after Nancy. "I hope not," she said with a worried frown.

They were on the way out of the office complex when they saw Bess, her long blond hair swinging over her shoulders as she bobbed her head in animated conversation with a security guard.

"It's after hours, miss," he was saying as Nancy and George hurried up. "Nobody's supposed to be in there after six o'clock."

Bess pulled herself up to her full five-feet-four inches, plumping up the shoulder pads of her red jacket in an effort to look authoritative.

"Here are my friends. They'll tell you. We have permission to be here."

"There're more of you? What's going on here?" asked the guard, who was beginning to sound aggravated.

"We've been up in Councilman Terry's office working on the voter-registration drive," said George.

"We're on an urgent errand," Nancy explained. "It could be a matter of life and death."

"Tell me another one." The guard moved to block the glass doors that led to the elevator and the underground garage where Nancy had parked her car. "I'm supposed to be notified of any nonofficial people on the premises after hours. I'm going to have to call the councilman about this."

"Of course you are," Nancy said quickly, cutting off George's protest before she could utter it. "You have to do your duty. In fact," she said, thinking fast, "that's just what I want to talk to you about."

Bess had a sheaf of flyers in her arms. Nancy grabbed a handful.

11

"River Heights really needs the help of a man like you who knows what has to be done and does it."

The guard had his mouth open to respond but couldn't get a word in.

"I want you to take these." Nancy pressed the flyers into his hands. He tried to push them away, and a few fell to the floor. "Oh, don't let those get damaged—they are *crucial* to the future of our community."

Looking bewildered, the guard stooped to retrieve the flyers, and Nancy gestured for Bess and George to move around him to the glass doors. "Thank you, thank you. You don't realize what a service you're performing for the public," she said. "I've got to run—good night."

Waving a cheerful goodbye, Nancy left the guard with his mouth hanging open and hurried to catch up with Bess and George. Her heart was beating fast. "Keep moving," she said.

"What was that?" asked Bess. "Some kind of comedy routine?"

"Something like that," said Nancy.

"What's the joke?" Bess looked confused. "I want to be in on it too."

"Don't worry. You're in on it." George grabbed Bess with one hand and shoved her along with the other. "But if you don't run as fast as you can right now, we'll all get stuck here cooling our heels till that outfit you're wearing has gone out of style."

"What's happening?" Bess scurried along as George nudged her to move faster.

"Don't talk. Run," said Nancy.

They'd left the guard in a pool of paper but knew he wouldn't be far behind.

They reached the elevator, and Nancy jabbed at the Down button. She doubted they'd have time to wait for it to arrive though.

She could hardly believe it when she heard the *whoosh* of the elevator doors parting. All three girls stormed the elevator, nearly mowing down a woman with a maintenance cart who was trying to get out.

"Sorry, ma'am. We have to take you out of your way for a minute," said Nancy as the woman opened her mouth to complain.

She saw the security guard rushing toward them and jabbed the Door Close button. The brushed steel portals eased shut just in time to keep him on the other side while George assured the cleaning woman that this really was an emergency, and—no, she wasn't being taken hostage.

Moments later they were in Nancy's blue Mustang, racing toward Kathy Novello's. The evening traffic rush had subsided and they were making fairly good time.

As they drove, Bess was filled in on what Nancy had overheard. "Nancy!" Bess wailed. "You're the only person I know who could turn stuffing envelopes into trouble. Believe me, this is going to become another case."

"I hope you're wrong," Nancy replied grimly.

They pulled up in front of a grimy brick building and jumped out of the car.

Kathy's apartment building wasn't in the best part of town, and it didn't have an elevator. The yellowing card by her downstairs doorbell said she lived on the third floor. Nancy and George took the stairs two at a time while Bess brought up the rear, puffing with each exertion. As they reached the third-floor landing, they heard a distant clatter, as though someone was clanging garbage-can lids together outside.

"Oh, no," George gasped as she dashed to the door with Kathy's apartment number on it.

Nancy's heart sank—the door to Kathy Novello's apartment was slightly ajar. That looked like trouble. She doubted that a young woman living alone would leave her front door unlocked.

Nancy gingerly pushed the door farther open and called out, "Kathy, are you here?"

There was a single, drawn-out metallic clang in the distance but not a sound from inside the apartment.

"Maybe she went out," George suggested.

Nancy didn't answer. She pushed the door wide and looked around the living room. It wasn't fancy: the furniture was worn and faded, and the off-white walls looked as if they could use a fresh coat of paint.

The window on the opposite wall had been pushed all the way up. Nancy walked over to it and looked out, down through the metalwork of a fire escape.

The body of a woman was lying facedown on the pavement below. Nancy knew from the grotesque angle of the figure that the person was dead.

"Oh, no."

It was the second time George had made that exclamation in the past few minutes. She was leaning out the window beside Nancy, and the shocked expression on her face told Nancy her guess had been right.

It was the body of Kathy Novello.

Nancy and her friends had just started telling their story to Detective Hicks when the ambulance pulled up with its siren wailing and lights flashing.

Nancy told the detective about the conversation she'd overheard in the councilman's office, and he wrote it all down, but instead of leaping into action, he remained in Kathy's apartment and questioned George about Kathy. George told him that Kathy had been dissatisfied with her job and that she'd also just broken up with her boyfriend.

Detective Hicks snapped his notebook shut. "Well, ladies, I'd say we've got a tough case here," he said, wearily massaging the back of his neck. "It seems to me that three scenarios are equally possible."

"Excuse me," Nancy said, trying not to sound impatient. "What are the three possible scenarios?"

Hicks walked over to the window. "One, Ms. Novello was murdered. Two, it was an accidental death. She slipped and fell. Or, three, she killed herself. In light of what this young lady"—he gestured at George—"has been telling me, I'd say suicide is as good a possibility as either of the others."

Leaning out, he called down for an officer to come up from the alley. "I want to see if they found anything unusual down there."

"But—" Nancy began to say, when she heard a sound that brought her bolt upright in her seat. She hurried over to the window.

One of the policemen below had reached up and grabbed the extension ladder to the fire escape and pulled it down toward him. The corroded metal was clanking and squealing in response.

"That's what I heard!" she exclaimed. "When I was outside the door to this apartment, I heard metal clanking. It must have been the ladder."

"How long between then and when you got to the window?" asked Detective Hicks. He sounded skeptical, but at least she'd captured his attention.

"Not more than a minute," Nancy answered.

The detective pulled his pen out again. "But you didn't actually see anyone?"

"No, but there could have been time for whoever it was to get out of sight if what I heard was the ladder coming back up after someone had climbed down it."

"Did you hear footsteps running away?"

"No, I didn't hear anything like that." Nancy couldn't help but feel exasperated with this methodical man. While he asked all his questions, whoever had caused Kathy Novello to fall to her death was getting away. "What I *did* hear was metal—clanking metal."

"I'm not surprised that you did," said a voice from the window.

Nancy turned to see the police officer from the alley climbing into the room.

"I'll bet there was a lot of clatter when she hit those trash cans. They're scattered all over down there."

"I see," said Detective Hicks as he closed his notebook and put it away.

Nancy gritted her teeth. "Please listen to me. I know someone meant to hurt Kathy Novello. And now she's dead. There *has* to be a connection!"

Detective Hicks sighed. "I'm not saying you're wrong, Ms. Drew. But I have no evidence. I don't even know where to start looking for this murderer of yours! The department *will* look into it.

But it's going to take some time. Now if you'll excuse me, I've got some things to take care of. The sergeant here will take your phone numbers, in case we need to contact you again."

Nancy knew Hicks was doing his job. But she also knew that the longer the case waited, the colder the trail would get. She *couldn't* sit by and do nothing while a murderer got away!

Bess had been right, she realized. She had found trouble—and she was in the middle of another case.

A half hour later the girls were still sitting in Nancy's car in front of Kathy's apartment building. Nancy couldn't bring herself to drive away with the cause of Kathy Novello's death hanging unresolved. Yet, she didn't know what else to do.

"You have to agree with Hicks that a conversation you accidentally overheard really isn't solid evidence," said George.

"I know it isn't," Nancy conceded, more discouraged than ever. "If I could just establish that there was a specific motive for those men to want Kathy out of the way—"

"You'd have to know what was on the piece of paper they were after."

"Right. And— Wait a second! *We* were the last people to use the copier. It could have gotten mixed in with the flyers we were copying," said Nancy, suddenly feeling revived.

A lead at last! This could be the starting point.

"Did either of you see an odd piece of paper mixed in with the flyers?" she asked eagerly.

"It wasn't in the pile we used for stuffing envelopes. I'm almost positive of that," said George.

"If it was in the tray of the machine before we started making copies then it would have ended up on the bottom of the first batch we did. What happened to that batch?"

"I took it," Bess chimed in. "I just hope I didn't leave off the paper you want at one of those stores I visited. I think I just handed out the ones off the top of the pile, but—"

"No 'buts' about it," said Nancy triumphantly. She'd been rummaging among the flyers Bess had tossed on the back seat when they jumped into the car. "Bless your heart, Bess. You dealt those flyers straight off the top of the deck, and look what we have here."

Nancy brandished the single sheet of paper that didn't match the rest.

"The motive!" she said.

Chapter

Three

THIS HAS TO BE what those men were after," Nancy went on, her eyes sparkling.

George and Bess pressed over Nancy's shoulder to get a look at the piece of paper that seemed to have caused the death of Kathy Novello.

"What is it?" asked Bess.

"Looks like a copy of a computer printout page," said George.

"It has something to do with the Immigration and Naturalization Service," Nancy added, skimming the contents. "And it looks as if somebody had folded over the upper right-hand corner before copying it. It has something to do with a Michael Mulraney."

"I know that name," said George. "I filed some papers about him at the councilman's office."

"Immigration papers?" asked Nancy.

"No, nothing like that. These files had to do with municipal contracts. Mulraney owns a contracting business—he was bidding on a job for the city."

"What does Councilman Terry have to do with that?" asked Nancy.

"He heads up an oversight committee to make sure the city doesn't hire any crooked contractors. A lot of towns have gotten into serious scandals over kickbacks and faulty work. Some have even been cheated out of millions. Tim Terry is determined not to have anything like that happen here."

"You're really stuck on this guy, aren't you?" asked Bess from the back seat.

"I'm not in love with him, if that's what you mean—I just think he's a good guy. What's wrong with that?" George sounded a little defensive.

"What did the oversight committee find out about Mulraney?" Nancy asked quickly.

"I don't have any idea. I was just helping out with the filing. That kind of information is confidential."

"Yes, I suppose it would be." Nancy thought a moment longer. "Do you know how to get in touch with him?"

"Mulraney? He has an office on the outskirts of town, if I remember right. I'm sure he's listed in the phone book. What are you planning, Nancy?"

21

"I feel a sudden urge to interview a building contractor," said Nancy, turning the key in the ignition and listening as the Mustang rumbled to life. "Maybe that committee found out something that wasn't quite legitimate about the way Mr. Mulraney does business."

"But he got the job."

"What?" Nancy had been about to pull out but hesitated instead.

"The city accepted Mulraney's bid, and he was given the contract," said George. "Nothing very big, as I remember. Nothing that would be worth risking jail for. And what would it have to do with immigration anyway?"

"I don't know, but there has to be a connection somewhere. I'm going to find it."

With a single, deft turn of the wheel, Nancy pulled the Mustang away from the curb. "If either of you sees a pay phone, yell," she said over her shoulder.

"Aaaaagh!" Bess cried promptly.

Nancy smiled. Count on Bess to bring a little lightness to any situation. "Thanks."

Michael Mulraney's answering service said he was still on the job, though it was nearly eight o'clock.

When the girls arrived at the construction site, they found him in the middle of inspecting the day's work. He was of medium height and compactly built; casually dressed in jeans and a blue work shirt, he could easily have been mistaken for one of his workers. As he held a portable work lamp aloft, Nancy saw thick, dark hair and blue eyes lit by its glow. He welcomed them with a wide, friendly smile.

"What can I do for you ladies?" He gestured toward the two-story duplex under construction behind him. "If you're interested in renting one of these places once they're built, I can give you the name of the agent."

Nancy barely registered the words he'd spoken. She was too busy listening to his voice, which was unusually deep. Could it be the one she'd heard earlier in the copy room? Her heart beat a little faster.

"Are you doing this work for the city of River Heights?" she asked to give herself something to say while she chose her next move.

If this was the man from the copy room, she had good reason to believe his jovial greeting was just a front, and he should be handled carefully.

"No, it isn't. I don't start that job till next month. Did you read about it in the paper?"

"Actually, I work for Councilman Tim Terry. I heard about it there," George chimed in.

Watching him, Nancy came to a decision. Knowing as little as she did about this case, she couldn't very well bluff her way through. Not when she didn't even know what she was trying to find out. She'd have to try shock treatment.

"I have something here that might interest you," she said, pulling the printout copy from her shoulder bag and holding it out for Mulraney to see.

If her purpose had been to break through Michael Mulraney's façade, then she had succeeded. He'd lifted the work lamp over the paper to read. His eyes were cast in shadow, but she could sense his whole body tensing suddenly. Nancy could feel anger there.

He grabbed for the paper with his free hand. Nancy whisked it out of reach just in time.

"Is that why the corner of the original is missing?" she asked. "Because you snatched it away from somebody?"

He'd moved the lamp, and she could see his eyes now. "Will you give me that?" he asked, the low tones of his voice rumbling. He was on the brink of rage. "It's my property after all."

"I'm not sure about that. I think I'd better keep it," Nancy said.

Mulraney glared at her. He wouldn't dare try anything in public, would he? Nancy wondered. She was suddenly glad she had her two friends there to back her up.

"Get off this site then," he said abruptly, "and don't come back."

His voice was different! Trying to conceal her surprise, Nancy stuffed the document into her bag and motioned for George and Bess to follow as she turned to leave. She remained silent as they walked back to the car.

"That sure didn't accomplish much," Bess said as she opened the door and climbed into the back seat.

"I'll say it didn't," George agreed. "What do you think, Nan?"

Nancy's hand was suspended in midair, with the key halfway to the ignition. She was staring out the window. She was remembering the deep voice she'd heard in the copy room.

"Earth to Nancy Drew. I asked what you thought," George repeated much louder.

"What? Oh. I don't think it was a bust at all," said Nancy. She fitted the key into the ignition. "We learned one very important thing."

"What did we learn?" asked Bess and George in unison.

"Well, both Mulraney and the man in the copy room have deep voices. In fact, they sound very much alike."

"But what does that tell us?" asked George. "Are they the same person?"

"Wouldn't you say that Mr. Mulraney was angry and upset?" asked Nancy.

"He sure was," answered Bess. "I thought he was going to try to make you into the Statue of Liberty, except you'd be carrying the lamp in your forehead instead of your hand."

"Well, the man at the councilman's office was

also very angry and upset," Nancy went on. "But did you notice what happened to Mulraney's speech when he got angry and upset?"

"Yes, I did," George piped up. "He started talking with an Irish brogue."

"That's right," said Nancy, "but the man in the copy room didn't have even a trace of an accent."

"So it wasn't Michael Mulraney you overheard today," George concluded.

"I don't think so."

"I'm glad that's cleared up," said Bess. "I think he's kind of cute."

"Good old Bess," said Nancy, smiling at her friend.

"But why did he get so mad when you showed him that piece of paper?" asked George.

"That's the other important thing," said Nancy, looking over her shoulder as she backed through the opening in the steel mesh fence that surrounded the construction area. "The one we *didn't* find the answer to."

But, she added to herself, tomorrow I can really start getting some answers.

The next afternoon Nancy was back home, lounging in the corner of the comfortable old couch in the den. She'd put on a blue skirt with a floral print and a white knit pullover, so she'd look neat and respectable when she went to the immigration office.

26

She was contemplating what kind of story she could tell there to get them to show her the intact version of the Mulraney document, when the front doorbell rang.

Nancy answered it and found herself face-to-face with the last person she expected to see on her front porch—Michael Mulraney.

"Uh—hi. What a surprise," Nancy said lamely. What was he doing there?

She noted with relief that the lock on the screen door was hooked. Although if Michael Mulraney wanted to, he could probably rip the door right off its hinges.

"I've come to apologize." He didn't sound angry, but Nancy remembered how quickly his mood had changed the night before. "One of my men who was working late recognized you last night. He told me you were a detective—he says you help people when they're in trouble."

"I try," she said, still cautious.

"I need you to help me with this."

He was holding a piece of paper up to the screen. There was a single sentence typed in the exact center, but Nancy couldn't make out what it said.

It took only a second for her curiosity to get the better of her caution. Opening the door, she stepped forward to read:

"The real Michael Mulraney is still alive."

Chapter

Four

Nancy read that surprising sentence through twice before looking up at Mulraney. His expression was very intense. She couldn't decide if that was good or bad.

"It's a complicated story," he said, "and I can't stay away from the job site for very long. My men think I've gone to lunch."

"At three in the afternoon?"

He shrugged. "Some of us work odd hours. That has something to do with my problem, actually. I can tell you about it out here on the porch if that's better for you."

His brogue had begun to set in. Whatever he had to say to her was obviously pretty important to him. Looking at him, Nancy saw nothing but distress on his face. Her instincts told her she had nothing to fear from Michael Mulraney.

"Let's talk inside," she said as she held open the screen door.

He followed her down the hall to the sunny, spacious kitchen. She offered him a seat and brought him a cola. He didn't relax much and sat on the edge of his chair.

Nancy and her guest weren't likely to be interrupted. Carson Drew was spending the week at a New York legal conference. And the Drews' housekeeper, Hannah Gruen, was out shopping for groceries, which usually took her hours.

"Would you like a sandwich or something?"

"Thanks, but no." He shook his head, then stared down at his callused, red hands.

"What does that note mean?" she asked, hoping to get him talking.

He looked up at her, and what she saw in his eyes touched her heart.

"It means that someone's found me out," he said in a lilting brogue. "Somebody knows I'm not really Michael Mulraney."

Nancy took the seat across the table from him. "Then who are you?"

He hesitated.

"You can trust me," she said softly.

"I have to trust someone, I guess." He pulled at the collar of his blue work shirt and sighed before going on.

"My real name is Kevin Dougherty, and I come from Belfast, Ireland. The part of Belfast they call the Bogside."

He said the name in a way that told Nancy he had no happy memories of the place.

"My family is still back there. Ever since I came to America three years ago, I've thought of nothing but getting them out and bringing them here, especially my brother. But he won't come without my mother and sisters. So I must make enough money to bring them all together."

He was staring at his hands again, his face clouded by troubles that were an ocean away.

"Why is it so important to you to bring your family here?" Nancy asked.

"Because the Bogside is no fit place to live," he said almost angrily. "The place is like a war zone. And there are no jobs, especially not for young men like my brother. I know what it's like to have no work to go to and nothing to do. It's easy to get in trouble when you have nothing to do."

"Is that what happened to you? Did you get into trouble back there?" That might explain why he'd changed his name.

"Not quite, but I came close. And my brother Jamie is closer even than I was. My mother writes me that he stays out half the night with a gang from the streets. I had friends that did the same thing, and they're in prison now."

His hands were clenched tight together, knuckles showing white through his deep tan. His eyes pleaded for her to understand.

"Don't you see? I had to do whatever was necessary to get them out of there."

"What exactly did you do?" Nancy asked carefully. Her heart went out to him. But she had to know more before making a final judgment.

"I pretended I was somebody else, somebody I thought was dead." He sighed again and sank back in his chair, as if he'd been deflated by the words.

"Tell me how you did that." Nancy encouraged him to continue.

He leaned forward once more. "I saved up for two years. The plane ticket from Dublin took most of that, but a friend of my mother's had come over to River Heights several years earlier, so I had a free place to stay. Then, my second day here I was offered a job as a carpenter, the work my father taught me before he died. I could hardly believe my good luck. Just the work I wanted to do, and so fast. But there was a problem."

Nancy had become wrapped up in his story. "What problem?" she asked.

"The foreman on the job said I had to have a social security number and a green card. All I had was a temporary visa. Then, my mother's friend came up with a solution."

"Who is this friend of your mother's?"

"Her name is Dee Shannon. She lives on the other side of town from here. Sometimes she rents out rooms—that's how she got the papers she gave me. They belonged to one of her roomers who had died." He deflated again. "At least, that's what she told me."

"And you used them to get a job under an assumed name?" Nancy asked. She could see how uncomfortable that question made him, but she had to know.

"Yes, I did," he said.

"Did you understand that it was illegal to pretend you were Michael Mulraney?"

He shuffled his feet under the table, looking miserable.

"I know it's hard for you to understand," he said. "I'd come here from a place where there was no chance for somebody like me. I truly believed that this job offer was a fluke, and if I passed it up there would never be another. So I became Michael Mulraney. Then, I worked day and night till I could get a small crew together and start taking jobs on my own. I just kept on working and saving and praying I wouldn't get caught."

Nancy nodded. "Have you saved enough to bring your family here?"

"Almost. This job for the city will give me the rest. Then they can come here and have a decent place to live and something to get started on. My father taught my brother carpentry too, so he can take over my business."

"And what about you?" Nancy asked.

"I'll turn myself in and take what's coming to me," Michael said with a heavy sigh.

"What do you think that will be?"

"They'll probably send me back to Ireland, but I won't mind if my family is taken care of." He tapped the note, which he'd tossed on the table next to the cola he hadn't touched. "Only now it looks like I'll be going back before they come here."

"So, you think this note is a threat of some kind?" Nancy said softly. She couldn't help feeling sorry about the fix he was in.

"I think whoever sent this is going to use what they know against me somehow," Michael answered. "I thought it must be you when I saw you with that immigration paper last night."

"But that paper doesn't say anything that could prove you're not Michael Mulraney," Nancy objected.

"The corner was folded over where the birth date should have been. The date was proof." Michael sighed once more. "The real Michael Mulraney is twenty-five years older than me. I think that the person who sent me this note has the original of that printout with the birth date still on it."

"What makes you so sure the note isn't just a friendly warning?"

"If they wanted to help me, wouldn't they tell me more than this?" He unfolded the paper to show her the one sentence again.

Kathy Novello's death made Nancy inclined to agree. Good Samaritans didn't push innocent secretaries out of windows. But did Michael Mulraney qualify as an innocent victim too? That wasn't clear.

"What is it you want me to do exactly?" Nancy asked, curious.

"Find out who sent this to me, and then we'll decide from there," he said quietly.

"I'll have to think about this," she said, looking away so she wouldn't see the hope fade from his eyes. "You broke the law, and I don't usually take on a case for anyone who's done that."

"I understand," he said, and she could tell he really did. That didn't make her decision any easier.

It was past suppertime when Nancy got to the pizza parlor. Bess was out, having finally maneuvered a date with Jeff Matthews, and it had taken Nancy an hour to track George down at the gym and wait for her to finish.

Under George's peaked hood, her dark curls were still damp from the shower as she sat in the booth across from Nancy and picked up a wedge of double-cheese with everything—except anchovies. She was wearing a gray, hooded sweatshirt jacket over a T-shirt and navy blue sweatpants.

Nancy shook her head in amazement. "You work out like crazy—then top it off with a million calories."

George's dark eyes twinkled. "I'm just making

sure I don't get carried away with this fitness stuff." She creased the wedge deftly down the middle so none of the ingredients would fall off, then wound a strand of mozzarella into the neat package. "Speaking of getting carried away, what's got you looking so serious?"

Nancy recapped her conversation with Mulraney. She had to talk to somebody, and she knew George could be trusted with his secret. She was well into her second slice by the time the story was finished.

"Let's think about what could happen," said George matter-of-factly. "If you don't take the case, he'll probably get caught and be sent back to Belfast. His brother will still be on the street, and the family will be back where they started."

"On the other hand," said Nancy as George twirled the pizza platter in search of the piece with the most goodies on it, "if I do take his case, Michael may be able to keep all of his hard work from going down the drain." She caught the edge of the platter in midtwirl. "And I'll have time to figure out what really happened to Kathy Novello."

Nancy bounced out of the booth, taking the platter with her.

"Where are you going with that?" cried George.

"I'm having it boxed to go. We've got something important to do."

Nancy tapped her keys on the counter while

the remains of their pie were wrapped up. "Thanks," she said briskly when it was done. "Let's go, George!"

Michael Mulraney was working late again. He saw the blue Mustang pull in and hurried over to greet Nancy and her friend.

"I didn't think you'd be coming to see me so soon," he said.

Nancy could tell he was very nervous. "I've made a decision," she said.

"I see." Mulraney shifted from one booted foot to the other. "Well?"

Nancy smiled warmly. "I'll take the case, but I need to get some more information from you. Do you have time to talk?"

Michael Mulraney looked relieved. "Sure," he said. "Just give me a minute to put the outside lights on."

Before Nancy could answer, he was off across the dirt yard.

She was getting out of the car when Michael suddenly went rigid beside the circuit breaker box. He began to twitch, first along his arms, then through his entire body.

Nancy gasped and ran toward him. "Come on!" she shouted over her shoulder at George. "He's being electrocuted!"

Chapter

Five

"Don't touch him, Nan! You'll get shocked too!" screamed George.

"I have to get him off that handle somehow!" Nancy tore away from her friend's grip on her arm and looked around her. There had to be something— "Wood!" she muttered, remembering that it was a nonconductor.

She pulled a two-by-four from a stack of lumber and thrust it at Michael, trying to pry him loose. He quivered some, but remained clamped fast to the circuit breaker.

"Harder!" cried George. "He's got a death grip on that switch."

She grabbed the board along with Nancy. They lunged forward together. The board struck Michael with a thud in the chest. *Whoosh!* The impact knocked the breath out of him.

At the same instant his hand popped off the charging handle. He slid to the ground, unconscious—but alive.

"Is he—is he all right?" asked George.

"Call an ambulance" was Nancy's only reply as she bent over Michael.

The lights had pulsed off and on while he held the shorting handle. Now they were out completely.

"What's going on?" called a workman who had come out of the building. Then he spotted Michael crumpled on the ground and Nancy hovering over him. "What happened to Mike?" the workman shouted in alarm.

"He got a heavy jolt from that circuit breaker. I'm trying to bring him around."

She slapped Michael's cheeks and called to him, but he didn't come to. Meanwhile, the workman was examining the circuit breaker box, being careful not to get too close. Nancy jumped up to peer over his shoulder.

"This thing is wired all wrong," the man said, sounding amazed. "There should be a negative and a positive here, but look"—he pointed—"there're two positives instead."

"What does that do?" Nancy asked. She bent down to listen to Michael's respiration. He was breathing steadily, but he still showed no sign of waking up.

"It means that, instead of alternating like it's supposed to, the current went around in a circle," the workman answered, making hand motions to demonstrate. "When Michael touched the handle he became part of that circle with the current going straight through him. It's a miracle he's still alive."

"Could those wires have been rigged wrong by accident?" Nancy asked.

"I don't see how. They were fine earlier."

"Then you think somebody must have switched the wires deliberately?"

"I don't think anything!" the man snapped, suddenly on the defensive. Then he hesitated. "Still, I don't see any other way it could have happened." He eyed her with suspicion. "Who are you, anyway?"

"I'm Nancy Drew. Who are you?"

"The name's Pete Donaldson. I'm Mike's foreman." He still sounded skeptical.

"Does Michael turn these outside lights on every night?" Nancy wanted to know.

"I guess he has done that, ever since the wiring was finished," said Pete.

"Is he usually alone on the job this late?"

"Usually, unless we have something big to finish. Sometimes I stay around, but most of the time he's alone," Pete answered.

Nancy nodded. Michael's routine would make him an easy target for a would-be enemy, she reflected. She knelt to check his pulse again. Rapid, but steady.

"Would you ever inspect this outside area, or

was Michael the only one who did that?" she asked, though she could already guess what the answer would be.

"He was the only one," said Pete. "Say, what's going on here?"

"I'm not sure what's going on," said Nancy. She debated what to tell him. Pete seemed to be exactly what he said, a guy who worked for Michael. Still, somebody with access to that box had rigged those wires, and Pete appeared to know how that would be done. She stood up.

"I suspect somebody's been trying to scare Michael," she went on, watching Pete carefully, "or maybe even kill him."

Pete stared.

"That's all I need," murmured an unsteady voice from the ground. Michael had regained consciousness.

He tried to sit up, but Nancy wouldn't let him.

A few minutes later the ambulance arrived and medics checked Michael over. They moved him to a cot in the construction trailer nearby. There'd been no serious damage done, except for the nasty bruises where Nancy and George had struck him with the board. The men tried to talk him into going to the hospital, but Michael wouldn't hear of it. Finally they left.

"All I need is a little rest," Michael said to Nancy. "And one *other* thing."

"What's that?" Nancy asked.

"To find out why someone would do something like this."

"We'll find out," replied Nancy seriously.

A broad grin lit up Michael's face, and he seemed to be a little less pale beneath his tan. He sat up painfully and grasped Nancy's hand. Then he looked dismayed and sank back down on the cot again.

"What's wrong?" she asked.

"I may have ruined our chance with the only lead we have," he said. "Yesterday, after I left your house, I was sure you were going to turn me down, so I thought I'd better check things out on my own.

"I went to see Dee Shannon, the woman who gave me Michael Mulraney's social security card. I'm afraid it didn't go very well."

George had been listening and looked suddenly worried.

"What do you mean?" Nancy asked Michael.

"My nerves were a bit on the ragged side. That's my only excuse for what happened," he said. "I lost my temper and started yelling at her for giving me the card in the first place." He hung his head. "Instead of getting information, I got kicked out and was told never to come back."

He looked so unhappy and ashamed of himself, and he'd been through so much in the past few days. Nancy couldn't bring herself to tell him that if he really had ruined their chances of getting Dee Shannon to cooperate, then they could really be in trouble. Michael Mulraney's hot temper might very well have cooked his own goose!

Late the next morning Nancy visited Mrs. Shannon. Michael had said she was a real TV buff and that it wasn't a good idea to interrupt her during the afternoon soaps or evening prime time.

She lived in a white, wood-frame house. Green flower boxes brimming with orange and yellow marigolds lined the wide porch. Dee Shannon answered the door, but it took some fast talking from Nancy to keep her from closing it again the minute Michael's name was mentioned.

"Please, believe me," Nancy pleaded, "Michael is in very serious trouble. You know him—normally he would never have acted the way he did yesterday."

"And you're asking me to get myself in trouble along with him?" Dee Shannon's naturally high-colored cheeks were even redder from the agitation of the moment. "After all, I'm the one who gave him that card."

"Why don't you let me in for a few minutes? We'll talk about what we can do to keep everybody out of trouble."

Mrs. Shannon was short and wide. She filled the doorway so Nancy couldn't possibly get past.

Instead of stepping aside, Mrs. Shannon moved back several steps, letting Nancy into the entryway but no farther. She knew she had to calm the woman down or they'd never be able to talk sensibly about Michael's situation.

"Something smells good," said Nancy. "Were you cooking?"

"Yes, I was."

"Don't let me stop you then," said Nancy with a bright smile. "I'll come into the kitchen and we can talk there while you cook."

Mrs. Shannon looked Nancy up and down suspiciously one more time, then turned and walked down the hallway.

"I do my cooking early so I can watch the soap operas when they come on," said Mrs. Shannon as Nancy surveyed the array of steaming kettles on the kitchen stove.

Nancy remembered what Michael had said about Mrs. Shannon being a real TV lover. Maybe that could be a way of getting to her.

"I met Rick Arlen once," said Nancy. "You know, the guy from 'Danner's Dream.'"

"You did?"

Nancy could see Mrs. Shannon beginning to thaw, and it wasn't because of the steamy kitchen.

"I can hardly watch that show since they had him die. It's just not the same without him."

Nancy nodded before steering the conversa-

43

tion back in the direction she wanted it to go. "Michael wishes he hadn't lost his temper with you."

"He shouldn't have talked to me the way he did." Mrs. Shannon sounded as if she was getting angry again.

"Well, he wasn't thinking straight at the time," Nancy said apologetically. She told Mrs. Shannon about Michael's problems.

"I think he snapped under the pressure," she finished up. "After all, he could lose everything."

Mrs. Shannon stared at her for a moment. "Yes," she said finally in a much softer tone. "I see what you mean."

Nancy tried not to let her sigh of relief be audible.

"I can't really help you much though," said Mrs. Shannon. "That other Mulraney—the real one—kept to himself. He didn't even eat his meals here the way most of my roomers do. Tall, handsome fellow—but not very memorable, for all that. He never smiled. He made it very clear that he minded his business and wanted everybody else to do the same. Then, the next thing I heard, he was dead, killed in some kind of construction accident."

Construction! That was the present Michael Mulraney's business too. Was it just coincidence, or was there more of a connection than that? Nancy realized she'd have to find out more about the first Mulraney.

"Did he have any friends that you know of?" she asked Mrs. Shannon.

"If he did, he never brought them here. He was quiet and neat, and he paid his rent on time. That's all I can tell you about him."

Nancy couldn't hide her sigh this time. It looked as if she'd hit a dead end.

"Wait a minute. Now that I think about it," said Mrs. Shannon, wiping her hands on her apron, "there was one thing I heard."

"What was that?" Nancy asked eagerly.

"Supposedly he hung around a pool hall in the neighborhood sometimes. It's called the Side Pockets Club." She frowned. "I remember it seemed strange to me. He struck me as too much of a gentleman for that crowd."

"Thanks, Mrs. Shannon," said Nancy. "I'll check it out."

"Don't you be going there by yourself," said Mrs. Shannon. For the first time, Nancy heard a bit of a brogue in the woman's voice. "As I understand it, that's no place for a young lady."

"Oh, it can't be that bad," Nancy protested, but Mrs. Shannon shook her head vigorously.

Mrs. Shannon wouldn't let Nancy go back into the hallway until she promised not to go alone. Nancy hated to deceive the woman, but it wasn't a promise she could keep.

However, when she saw the pool hall, she wondered if she shouldn't have taken Dee Shannon's advice.

The sidewalk in front of the Side Pockets Club was littered with bottles and cans. The windows of the one-story building had been painted over in dark green with black lettering. Nancy couldn't tell anything about what or who was inside. She remembered Mrs. Shannon's warning. Still, it was a bright, sunny afternoon, and Nancy was anxious to get on with the investigation. She was following a trail that had been cold for a few years, and she had the feeling it could get colder by the minute. She opened the door and stepped inside. It could have been midnight instead of broad daylight. The long, narrow room was lit only by green-shaded light bulbs suspended from the ceiling over a dozen or so pool tables. By the time Nancy's eyes had grown accustomed to the gloom, she heard someone move in behind her.

The man blocking the door was tall and dark-haired and was staring straight at her. Nancy looked around and saw more guys gathering, forming a semicircle with her at the center. She could feel their silent challenge fill the dimly lit room.

This was a scene she'd have to play just right, or she could be in *big* trouble!

Chapter

Six

"DOES ANYBODY HERE feel like shooting pool?" asked Nancy, trying to sound confident as she elbowed her way through the lineup of guys. She half wished she was back watching the soaps with Dee Shannon.

She could see that the swaggering character at the door had been thrown off guard by her question. He obviously didn't expect a "nice girl" like her to be a pool player. He watched as she made a ritual of selecting a cue from the brace on the wall. She took each one down and tested it for balance across her palm and for straightness by eyeing it along the shaft.

Nancy had learned to shoot pool in the billiard room of one of her father's lawyer friends several years earlier. She'd been at a very determined age and went back again and again until she got her technique down pat. She made a silent wish that all that practice would pay off now when she needed it most.

"First game is mine," said a stocky, tough-looking guy who had been leaning against a nearby table.

Nancy guessed from the way the others deferred to him that he was a leader here.

"What're we playing for?" he asked, looking her up and down.

"How about information?" Nancy answered.

"What kind of information?"

Nancy knew it was always safest to keep a half truth as close as possible to the whole truth.

"I'm trying to help out a guy I know," she said. Snickers rippled through the crowd, as if a girl like her was the last person a guy would turn to for help. She had to gain some respect and do it fast.

"My break?" she asked her opponent.

"Sure. Why not?" he said. "What's your name anyway? I don't like to shoot with anybody unless I know their name."

"Nancy Drew," she said, then wished herself luck and crouched down to line up her shot.

She stroked the cue complete with follow-through, just as her father's friend had taught her. There was a murmur of approval as several balls rumbled into the pockets, and she realized she'd been holding her breath since her shot. She let it out slowly so no one would notice.

"What should I call you?" she asked her opponent as she chalked her cue and forced herself to appear at ease. It wasn't easy, with a roomful of tough characters watching her.

"Ace."

She saw some knowing looks exchanged around the room and no snickers this time. She called her next shot and sank it.

"So tell us your story," said Ace.

"Like I told you before, I'm here to help a friend," she said, improvising a story rapidly. "In fact, he's from this neighborhood."

She walked slowly around the table, sizing up her next shot. Then she aimed and sank that one too. Still in her crouch, she peeked under her outstretched arm to check Ace's reaction. She had to be careful not to make him look foolish in front of his buddies, and being beaten by a girl could do just that. Yet she didn't want to cheat if she could help it.

"My friend is in pretty big trouble," she went on.

She tried to sound calm, but the situation was making her nervous. Her hand was shaking slightly as she took her shot. She missed, honestly.

"Let her take it over. She was shook up about her friend," said someone in the crowd.

"No thanks," Nancy answered quickly. "That's not my style."

There was another murmur of approval as she stepped back from the table. Ace looked a little guilty as he lined up his shot, but he took it anyway. To Nancy's great relief, the ball sped across the green felt and into the side pocket. Right then, she'd rather lean against the wall and watch Ace show off his moves.

"What is it you're trying to find out for this friend of yours?" he asked as he sauntered around the table, sizing up the position of the balls just as she had done.

"About the guy who's behind all his troubles," said Nancy.

"Don't you know any guys who could take care of this for you?"

"It isn't the kind of thing I can let other people know about, and he's counting on me."

"Since when does anybody count on a girl?" the character by the door piped up, and there were snickers again.

Nancy looked hard and straight into his sneering face, her stomach flip-flopping. She held her breath a minute before answering.

"Since I promised to help him," she said.

"All right," said Ace, clapping her shoulder as he sauntered past her toward the other end of the table. He turned to the guy by the door. "Now, let the lady tell her story, McCarthy," he said with a hint of a warning in his tone.

"How's *she* going to help someone?" McCarthy muttered. This time there were no answering snickers. He scowled and skulked back against the door.

"You got a name on this guy you're after?" asked Ace.

"Michael Mulraney."

Another murmur traveled around the room, and Ace straightened from his crouch to study her face for a moment before responding.

"I'm afraid you're a little late," he said. "Somebody beat you to the punch with that one. Old metal-mouth's dead and gone."

Metal-mouth, how odd, Nancy thought. She studied Ace. She'd swear he was telling the truth. As far as Ace knew, Mulraney was dead, just as Dee Shannon had said he was. Nancy didn't exactly know what she'd expected to find out, but she was disappointed.

"And you're lucky he *is* dead and gone," Ace added. "I don't care how tough you are, you wouldn't want to go up against Mulraney."

"Tell her what he did for a living," said McCarthy in his smart-aleck way from the sidelines.

"He was a professional." When Nancy showed no sign of comprehending, Ace went on. "He was a hitter."

"Yeah. He killed people for fun and profit," said McCarthy in a mocking tone. "From what I heard, he did it mostly for fun. Is that what he did to your boyfriend?"

51

"Not my boyfriend, my friend," she said as firmly as she could manage. Her mind was reeling. The further she delved into this case, the more dangerous it became. A hit man!

"Lay off, McCarthy," Ace warned.

Nancy could feel the tension between them.

"What happened to Mulraney?" she asked hastily to cool them down. The last thing she wanted was to end up in the middle of a brawl between these two.

"Word on the street was he did exactly what you claim he did to your friend. He let somebody down. Only this time he did it to the wrong dude, and that dude cashed in Mulraney's chips for him."

"Permanently," McCarthy added with a nasty smile.

"That's right," Ace confirmed. "There was a big construction project over on the west side at the time. Rumor was they dumped him into the foundation."

"How do you know that's true?" Nancy asked.

"Because nobody ever saw him again, and he left a lot of loose ends behind, the kind of stuff a guy would clear up if he had a chance to."

"What kind of loose ends?"

"Like people who owed him lots of money," McCarthy interrupted again. "And Mulraney always made a point of collecting his debts, one way or another."

"Did he have any friends?" Nancy asked Ace.

"Why do you want to know that?"

She heard the edge of suspicion in his voice. "I guess I want to hear the details to satisfy myself that he's really dead."

"You can take my word for it. He is. Mulraney was alive one night, hanging out on the street, acting like his usual miserable self. Next day he was history." Ace took the shot that clinched the game for him. "Besides, he was too mean to have friends."

Nancy looked crestfallen as the ball rolled into the trough. Since that was actually how she felt about what she'd learned so far, it wasn't too hard to pretend.

"Sorry," said Ace, sounding as if he really was.

"Good game," Nancy said.

She walked to the brace on the wall and hung up her cue, then extended her hand to Ace for a shake. He took it solemnly. "Any time," he said.

Nancy moved toward the door, but McCarthy stepped in front of her to block her way just as he had when she first came in.

"McCarthy, you called for winners, didn't you?" said Ace, chalking his cue and giving Nancy a conspiratorial grin. "That means you're up against me."

Nancy saw McCarthy's sneering façade slip a notch as mocking laughter rippled nearby. This was a weak moment for him, and she'd better take advantage of it. She walked around him to the door, paused a moment to salute Ace, then was outside the pool hall at last. She let out a long sigh of relief.

Walking to her car, Nancy thought about what she'd learned. It looked as if the original Michael Mulraney really was dead. Nobody'd seen a body, but that was probably how things were done in the circles he frequented.

She opened the door of her car and slipped gratefully inside. Her visit with Ace and company had left her more than a little tense. She switched on the ignition and pushed in the tape she had left in the deck. Maybe some music would help.

But instead of the song she'd expected, an all-too-familiar deep voice rumbled from the speakers. "You'd better watch your step, Nancy Drew!"

Nancy's hand dropped from the tape deck as she listened. It was the same menacing voice she'd heard that night from the copy room.

"You could get hurt—maybe you could even get *dead!*"

Chapter

Seven

Nᴀɴᴄʏ ᴅɪᴅɴ'ᴛ ʟɪᴋᴇ being threatened. She frowned. So the man with the deep voice knew who she was, and he thought he could scare her off. Well, she wasn't backing out now!

With a screech of her tires, she pulled out into the traffic and drove to the Municipal Building.

At Councilman Terry's office, George was in a planning meeting, so Nancy sat down to wait for her in the reception area. The receptionist smiled at her. "Are you coming to our big fund-raiser tomorrow night?" she asked Nancy.

"I don't know—am I invited?" Nancy asked, surprised.

"Oh, of course," the receptionist assured her. "Didn't George tell you? All the staff members are encouraged to bring a few guests. You know, the more money we can raise for the councilman's campaign, the better."

"I can see the logic." Nancy laughed. "The more the merrier, right?"

"Mmm-hmm." The receptionist nodded. "All of Mr. Terry's biggest backers are going to be there. Even Bradford Williams—he's coming from Chicago for it. He's such a *wonderful* man!" She looked slightly starry-eyed. "Handsome, generous . . ." Her voice trailed off as a door opened.

"Nancy! What are you doing here?" George walked over to them, looking crisp and business-like in her tailored jacket and slacks.

"I came by to ask your advice," Nancy said, trying to signal with her eyes that she needed to talk to George alone.

George winked. "Just call me Miss Lonelyhearts," she joked. "Let's talk on the way out. I got finished early today."

Saying goodbye to the receptionist, who seemed disappointed to lose her audience, Nancy and George headed to the elevators while Nancy repeated the details of her eventful afternoon.

The elevator doors eased open, and a young man of medium height with slicked-back black hair stepped out, moving fast and not bothering to look where he was going. His briefcase grazed Nancy's leg as he pushed past, but he didn't stop.

He turned to give her an annoyed look as if

she'd run into him instead of the other way around. Then he hurried on his way, hawk nose in the air, walking faster than ever in the direction of the councilman's office.

"Who was that?" asked Nancy, staring after him. Something about him struck a chord in her memory. Maybe it was just his unpleasantness. She was beginning to think this must be her day for running into unpleasant characters.

"His name is Franklin Turner," said George, grimacing. "He's one of Councilman Terry's aides."

"I thought politicians were in the business of making friends. Terry won't win any popularity contest by having that guy on his staff."

"Turner is what you might call a political appointee," George explained as they got on the elevator. "His parents are old friends of the councilman's family. The way I heard it, they want Turner to get into politics and thought working here would be great training for him, especially since the councilman's next stop will probably be Washington."

"From what I saw, Turner needs all the training he can get!"

"You're right about that. If he had to depend on his personality to get ahead, he'd be in big trouble," said George as they got off the elevator. "But, if it's any consolation, he's even less enthusiastic about being here than we are to have him.

The job doesn't interest him much. It was completely his family's idea."

"Hmm." Nancy couldn't feel much sympathy for someone whose parents' money was greasing his way into public service.

"Punctuality isn't one of his strong points either," said George, checking her watch. "Three o'clock, and he's just getting to the office. He was probably out late last night. I hear he loves the Chicago club scene."

"Hmm," said Nancy once more. "Well, he sounds pretty awful. Let's not talk about him anymore. Is there a pay phone around here? We should call Bess and see if she wants to help out."

It was time to get down to some hard-nosed investigating of the Michael Mulraney case. They gave Bess a call, but she wasn't home, so Nancy and George were on their own.

There was just time for George to get to the newspaper office and check the articles morgue before it closed for the day. Maybe she could find something about the accident that killed the original Mulraney.

Meanwhile, Nancy went to the police station to see if she could find out what was going on with the investigation into Kathy Novello's death. Though she wasn't hopeful, there was always a chance that Detective Hicks had turned up something she could use.

"We did the standard follow-up, looked the

place over, talked to the neighbors," he said. "We didn't find a thing. We're still doing background checks on her, but so far we've come up blank everywhere."

Of course Nancy wasn't about to give up that easily.

"Was there anything unusual about any of the neighbors you questioned?" she asked.

"The guy downstairs seemed disappointed that he had been out at the time and missed the excitement."

"Would you mind giving me his name?"

Hicks squinted at her. "Unofficially, all right? Norman something." He shuffled through some papers in his Out basket. "Norman Fredericks, but I'm telling you he's no lead. He doesn't know anything. He wasn't even around when it happened."

"You're probably right," said Nancy.

But whatever Hicks might say, she intended to have a talk with Mr. Fredericks.

"I didn't find out a thing," said George when they met at the pizza parlor later. They couldn't find Bess—she was probably out with her new heartthrob again. "There's no record of Mulraney's death—or of his life either, for that matter."

"Interesting," murmured Nancy, half to herself.

"What's so interesting about it?" asked George as she contemplated her hero sandwich unenthusiastically. "Seems pretty much like running into a blank wall to me."

"First of all, this makes it look like the guys at the Side Pockets Club could be right about how Mulraney died, and Dee Shannon was probably lied to."

"How do you know that?" George delicately popped a shred of lettuce into her mouth.

"The fact that there's no record suggests to me that it could have been a contract killing after all, a professional hit with no loose ends and no trace left behind. If his death was a simple accident, as Mrs. Shannon said, it would have been reported in the paper." Nancy took a sip of her diet soda while she thought a moment. "Even so, she could be partly right. Both Mrs. Shannon and the Side Pockets guys said his death had something to do with a construction site."

George and Nancy looked at each other.

"And the *new* Michael Mulraney is in the construction business," said George slowly.

Nancy nodded unhappily. She knew George was thinking what she herself had tried to avoid thinking. She liked Michael Mulraney and wanted to believe he was just a hard-working guy struggling to help his family. She didn't want to believe that struggle had made him so desperate he might have killed for it. She picked up her shoulder bag and started fishing for the keys to her car.

"I think we'd better get on with this investigation," she said.

George looked down at her half-eaten hero. "Don't bother saying it. I know the routine." She sighed out loud. "I'll have this wrapped to go."

Norman Fredericks lived on the second floor, directly below Kathy Novello's apartment. He needed no softening up to talk.

"I keep a close watch on things around here. I guess you might say it's my main form of entertainment," he admitted.

Glancing around the barren apartment, Nancy could believe he needed to look elsewhere for his interests.

"Some people watch television," he said, "but I prefer real life. Then I can use my imagination to make up the bits that go between the little pieces I see." He was small and very thin with pale, wispy hair.

"What pieces did you see of Kathy Novello's life?" Nancy asked.

"Nothing much, really. She was very quiet. I had to do a lot of imagining where she was concerned, but I never thought up anything like what ended up happening to her."

Nancy could hear in his voice the disappointment Detective Hicks had mentioned. She was disappointed too. Norman would have made an excellent witness, but he said he hadn't witnessed anything.

"I did see something yesterday," he added. "I might call the police about it and I might not. They wouldn't even take the time to come inside and talk while they were here, and they wouldn't tell me a thing about what was going on. So why should I tell them what I saw?"

"If you'd like to, you could tell *us* what you saw," Nancy suggested, trying not to sound too eager. "We came in and talked."

"Yes, you did," he said, looking her over thoughtfully for a moment. "I suppose I could tell you.

"Well"—he leaned forward in his seat— "there was this young man in the hallway, and I'm almost certain I heard him upstairs trying the Novello girl's door, but the police had put on a special lock so he couldn't get in."

"Did you actually see him?" asked Nancy.

"Yes, I did," Fredericks answered, his tiny eyes glittering at the prospect of having an interested audience at last. "He was about medium height. And he had black hair. I only saw him from the back." He looked disappointed. "But from the way he stomped out he seemed pretty upset."

Nancy's heart sank. "I see," she said. Standing up, she held out her hand. "Thank you for your time, Mr. Fredericks. You've been a big help."

Later, as they were walking away from the

building, George said what they'd both been thinking.

"You know who that description sounds like, don't you?"

"Yes, unfortunately, I do."

"Michael Mulraney."

Nancy nodded agreement, though she wished she didn't have to.

"Maybe we should call him Kevin Dougherty," George remarked.

"Whatever we call him, we'd better do it while we're asking him some tough questions about where he was the night Kathy Novello died. And there's no time like the present for doing that."

Nancy hurried toward her car with George in her wake. She didn't bother calling Michael's answering service this time. She figured he'd be at the job site.

But when she pulled up to the curb, the steel link gates were closed and locked and a small crowd had gathered outside.

"What's going on?" George asked.

Nancy parked as fast as she could, half in and half out of the space, and both girls rushed to the gate. They could see that the outside lights were off around the building once again.

"There's been an accident in there," a woman carrying a grocery bag volunteered. "They say a big scaffolding collapsed and somebody got killed!"

Chapter
Eight

THE WAIL of an ambulance siren told Nancy this was no narrow escape like the incident with the circuit breaker. The gate swung open to let the ambulance pass. Nancy grabbed George's hand and they slipped inside.

They found Pete Donaldson, and Nancy repeated George's question. "Michael was up on the scaffolding correcting a mistake in some window trim when the support rope broke," the foreman explained. "He doesn't usually wear a safety belt. Thank heaven, he had one on tonight. That belt saved his life."

Nancy had kept her distance from the spot where the ambulance team was huddled around the dark-haired form on the ground. Now she pressed forward to make certain that Pete was right and Michael was safe.

64

"He was lucky in another way too," said Pete. "That block and tackle over there came down just inches from his head. If that had hit him he'd be dead now for sure."

While Michael was being lifted into the ambulance, Nancy went to take a closer look at that scaffolding cable. Unfortunately, there was no way of telling if it had been tampered with. If someone had cut this cable partway through, then they'd done so strand by strand to make it look like a fray.

"Excuse me," Nancy said to one of the paramedics. "Is he going to be all right?"

The paramedic looked at her. "Friend of yours?" she asked. "Sure, he'll be just fine. We'll take him in for observation, but I'll bet you he'll be on his feet again tomorrow. Don't worry." She gave Nancy and George a reassuring smile, then climbed into the back of the ambulance.

Nancy frowned. So far Michael had had two near misses. True, he'd survived both, but either could easily have been fatal. He couldn't possibly have arranged them, could he?

No, it seemed highly unlikely. And even if it was possible, Nancy couldn't believe it. Her instincts kept insisting that Michael was the victim, not the villain here.

So then who *was* the villain? Who had caused Kathy Novello's death—and who was trying to kill Michael now?

Just then something that had been nagging at

the edge of Nancy's consciousness leapt into focus. She grasped George's arm and pulled her friend around to face her.

"Remember the description Norman Fredericks gave of the man he saw at his apartment building?" she said urgently.

"Sure I do."

"Well, could it fit somebody else besides Michael? What about someone Kathy knew from the office?"

George paused a moment to think. Then her eyes widened. "She had a crush on Franklin Turner," she said, staring at Nancy. "And he fits that description too."

Nancy nodded. "I thought there was something familiar about him when I saw him this afternoon," she said. "I just figured out what it was. I saw the profile of the guy who was being threatened in the copy room. It looked a lot like Turner's."

"But he's such a—such a wimp!" George protested. "Could he kill someone?"

"I don't know," Nancy said grimly. "But I'm going to find out."

Nancy, Bess, and George spent the next morning at the hospital. Michael was being discharged, and Nancy had volunteered to drive him home.

"Do you really think this guy Franklin Turner could be involved in Kathy's death and what's happening to Michael too?" asked Bess as they waited.

"Why not? He had access to the copy machine. It could have been him I overheard that night threatening to take care of Kathy. And it was Michael's document he was after."

"But Turner's rich! Why would he need to blackmail someone like Michael?" George asked, looking doubtful.

"We don't know for sure that this *is* a case of blackmail," said Nancy. "We're not sure yet what's going on. There hasn't been any demand for money. In fact, whoever is doing these things to Michael seems to want him out of the way permanently, and that's no way to get somebody's money."

"That's true," said George with a grim smile. "But then, the question is, why would Franklin Turner want Michael Mulraney out of the way?"

"I don't have an answer to that yet." Nancy was well aware that her theory had gaping holes in it, and she was a long way from filling them.

"I'm not saying I don't think Turner could do such a thing. He strikes me as one of those rich kids who thinks he can get away with anything," George commented. "Still, he'd have to have a reason."

"I agree. I think it's time for a closer look at Franklin Turner. Will he be at that fund-raiser tonight?"

George shrugged. "I guess so."

"I think Councilman Terry just found another supporter," said Nancy with a smile.

"Hey! I want to go too," Bess chimed in. "Is it a formal?"

"If you're talking about a party, how about inviting me along?"

The girls looked up to see Michael Mulraney limping toward them, grinning rather crookedly. His right arm was in a soft sling, and he appeared to be listing in that direction.

"You don't exactly look like you're up to celebrating," said George skeptically.

"Could you deny a condemned man his final wish?"

There was that crooked grin again. Nancy tried to smile along with him but couldn't. The events of the past few days hadn't put her in the right frame of mind to appreciate that kind of humor.

They all dressed in their best for the Pinnacle Club. George had on a navy blue dress with a short white jacket that emphasized her slim figure.

Nancy's two-piece outfit was just the right color blue to set off the shine of her red-blond hair and put a blush in her cheeks.

"What a place!" Bess said as they entered the elegant foyer. She paused and stared at the gleaming chandeliers and marble columns. "I bet there'll be a lot of great-looking guys here too!"

"I thought you were only interested in Jeff Matthews," Nancy said, teasing her a bit.

Bess smoothed the skirt of her yellow silk dress. "Well, he's wonderful, of course," she replied. "But he's not the only guy in the world. Anyway, I can look, can't I?" she added with a mischievous grin.

George laughed. "Poor Bess. Being in love is almost as hard as being on a diet, huh?"

Nancy looked around curiously. She was only interested in one guy tonight, and Franklin Turner was hardly great looking. But she didn't care as much about looking at him as listening to him. She was certain she'd recognize his voice if it was the one she'd overheard in the copy room.

There was a sudden clatter behind her, and she turned to see a half-dozen nails bouncing across the parquet floor.

"Sorry," said Michael, retrieving the hardware and stuffing it into his suit pocket. "I stopped off at the site on my way here, and I guess I brought some of the job along with me."

They moved into the main gallery where the reception had already started.

"I hadn't expected anything quite this fancy for a local politician," Nancy remarked.

"I don't think he'll be local for long," said George. "I hear he's planning to run for Congress soon—maybe even the Senate."

"Does he have the kind of support it takes to do that?" Nancy asked.

"That's what he's after here tonight."

"These are mostly businesspeople, aren't they?" asked Nancy. She'd recognized several associates of her father's.

"That's right," said George and began pointing out the big names. "We're expecting some potential backers from as far away as Chicago."

"So I heard at the office yesterday."

"I wish businessmen were younger," lamented Bess, still scanning the crowd.

Nancy laughed. "It takes a few years to get this successful."

"There's one closer to our age, but he's not exactly my type."

Nancy looked across the room where Bess was pointing. It was Franklin Turner!

He wore a tuxedo, and he had a very sophisticated-looking young blond woman on his arm.

"There's Turner," said George, who'd made the same discovery.

"Who's that with him?" asked Nancy, adjusting the jacket of her blue outfit and wondering how she'd look in a sleek black number like the one Turner's date was wearing.

"One of his friends from Chicago, probably. He doesn't have much to do with anybody from River Heights. Not unless they're very important, that is," said George. "See those two men he's walking up to? They're big-time lawyers, Jethro Serkin and Maxwell Edwards. Turner's probably trying to convince them he's running the councilman's operation single-handedly."

Nancy had heard Carson Drew mention both of those names. She wished he were here, so he could refresh her memory.

"We got word today that Jethro Serkin wants to cosponsor the voter-registration drive," said George proudly.

"Congratulations," said Nancy. She was only half paying attention, because she'd been watching Franklin Turner.

Two other men had joined his circle, and Nancy was about to ask George who they were when Councilman Terry and his wife came up to introduce themselves to Nancy and Bess.

They had a good talk until the councilman stopped in midsentence as a distinguished-looking man entered the room. Terry excused himself without finishing whatever he'd been saying and hurried away with his wife in tow.

"Bradford Williams just came in," said George, nodding toward the new arrival. "He was one of the people we were hoping would come tonight." There was a flash of gold as Williams smiled down at Mrs. Terry.

"He's nice-looking," Bess commented through a mouthful of pâté. She'd sent Michael after a waiter with a tray. "How old is he?"

"Old enough," George answered dryly.

Meanwhile, on the other side of the room, the group Nancy was interested in had dissolved.

Maxwell Edwards was talking to someone she'd never seen before, and she couldn't find Franklin Turner.

"I'll see you later, guys. There's something I have to do," said Nancy, and she launched herself into the crowd.

She moved purposefully through the two rooms, looking for the distinctive silver-blond hair of Turner's companion. She'd be easier to pick out in a crowd than he was, but neither of them was anywhere. Nancy even checked the ladies' room. She should have guessed from what George had said about him that Turner might not stay too long at a party with what he would consider local yokels.

"There you are," said George, hurrying up to Nancy as she emerged from the ladies' room. "Gee, it's great to be friends with the daughter of the famous Carson Drew. I have a feeling that's why we got this." She held up an elaborately hand-lettered card of heavy, cream-colored vellum.

"What is it?" Nancy asked.

"An invitation to a private supper given by Terry and his wife for their special friends and associates. They're picking us up outside and we're being driven there in a limousine."

"All of us?" asked Bess, who had just walked up with Michael. "Right now?"

"That's what it says," George answered.

Nancy really wasn't in the mood for another party. Then a thought occurred to her.

"Will Franklin Turner be there?" she asked.

"I wouldn't be surprised."

That made up Nancy's mind and the mention of the limo had sold Bess on the idea. Michael agreed to tag along.

Bess was in seventh heaven as the long, sleek car eased away from the portico of the Pinnacle Club.

"I absolutely love limos," she exclaimed, as she explored the backseat cabinet. It was equipped with a television, CD player, and fully stocked bar.

Bess had served them each a soda with crushed ice in a crystal glass and was starting on the assortment of munchies when the car pulled over to the side of the road. The outside view was mostly obscured by the black glass and surrounding darkness, but Nancy could tell they'd left town and were on a country road.

The partition between the front and back seats was made of heavy, opaque Plexiglas. It was closed as it had been from the start. It occurred to Nancy that the Pinnacle Club doorman had helped them into the car, and they'd never actually seen their driver.

She had her hand on the intercom button when an all-too-familiar deep voice came through the speaker.

"End of the line" was all it said.

Nancy heard the front door on the driver's side open and slam shut. She pressed herself up against the window, but could make out only an indistinct form hurrying toward another car up ahead. The figure climbed in and drove away.

"What's going on?" asked George.

Nancy didn't answer. With rising dread she reached for the door handle and pulled it. The door didn't budge.

"Nancy, what's happening? Why are we stopped?" Bess asked, alarmed at the look on her friend's face.

Michael sniffed the air. "What's that smell?" he cried.

Nancy swallowed hard. "Guys, I think we're in trouble," she said. "That's the car's exhaust— and it's loaded with carbon monoxide!"

Chapter

Nine

EXHAUST FUMES WERE HISSING steadily into the car. Bess opened her mouth to scream, but the sound was choked off as she started to cough.

Nancy knew they had to remain calm and act fast. Carbon monoxide didn't take long to knock a person out.

"Give me your sling," she said to Michael.

He winced as he yanked off the piece of black cloth and handed it over. Nancy grabbed the seltzer spigot from the wet bar. Her eyes had begun to water. She had to concentrate just to see clearly.

"Let us out of here!" shouted Bess between choking sounds. She started pounding on the door.

"Don't panic!" said Nancy in a voice so stern

and loud it made Bess snap around to look at her. "And don't waste your energy beating on a locked door."

She barely got that out before her first fit of choking overtook her. Time was dwindling now. Once the coughing turned to spasms she'd have a hard time doing anything.

She saturated the sling with seltzer water and handed it to George. "Tear this into four pieces and give each of us one," Nancy instructed. "We'll put them over our faces and breathe through them."

"Let me," said Michael tensely.

"You can't tear cloth with one hand. Anyway, I need you for something else." It was getting harder for Nancy to speak now. "Do you have any tools with you?"

She remembered the nails falling from Michael's pockets in the foyer of the Pinnacle Club and prayed they weren't all he'd stashed away. Michael rummaged in his pockets and pulled out a four-inch level. The bead of yellow liquid at its center bounced crazily in Nancy's blearing vision as she shook her head vigorously.

"Something to get us through to the front."

She gestured at the partition between the seats. They had to get to the controls up there. The doors and windows were electrically controlled, and the controls had to be in the front.

Bess had taken off her shoes and was pounding on the back and side windows with them. It was a futile gesture, but Nancy didn't tell her that. She'd seen the tears streaming down her friend's face and knew they weren't just from irritated eyes. Bess was terrified.

George handed out the pieces of wet material. Nancy slapped hers over her nose and mouth and breathed in. The bubbles from the seltzer tickled her nose, but the mask did help her to breathe. And at this point, every little bit helped.

Meanwhile, Michael's foraging had produced a tape measure, a notebook and pencil, and more nails. Then from his inside jacket pocket he pulled a small screwdriver. Nancy gestured toward the mechanism that held the partition window in place, and Michael started prying at the clasp. When Bess heard Michael chiseling at the lock, she spun around.

"I'll help," she choked as she scrambled across the seat, clambering over George. Before Nancy could comprehend what was happening, Bess had grabbed the screwdriver handle along with Michael and gave it a furious jerk.

Extreme fear can make a person very strong all of a sudden. And that had happened to Bess. Fueled by terror, the force of her pull on the handle was too much for the screwdriver. The long blade snapped with a crack that made Nancy sick to her stomach.

Michael wrestled the handle away from Bess and went on jabbing at the lock with what was left, but Nancy could see it wouldn't do any good.

"Spray!" she choked at George, gesturing toward their nose cloths.

George spritzed them each with another dousing of seltzer. The dancing bubbles didn't feel like tingles this time. They burned like tiny, hot needles searing Nancy's nostrils.

Still, that wasn't what worried her most. She could feel herself getting woozy. She knew how dangerous it could be to slow down in a situation like this. Fast thinking was more crucial than ever.

A clever idea was desperately needed to save them from what was beginning to look more and more like their fate. But no idea came.

Nancy felt her muscles growing slack despite her efforts to keep them taut and action-ready. Bess was racked with choking spasms now. She sounded as if she was on the verge of strangling, and George and Michael would not be far behind.

Nancy had to think! Her powers of reasoning and deduction had been her mainstay in times of trouble for as long as she could remember. They were clearly failing her now as she felt herself fading from consciousness.

The gas had slowed the others down too. Bess

was back at the window, but the results were closer to tapping than pounding now.

Then, through the fog of Nancy's gas-clogged thinking, came the faint glimmer of an idea.

"Backs against the seat!" she rasped as she plopped back onto the cushioned leather that had seemed so luxurious such a short while ago.

The other three stared at her instead of moving. Their brains were obviously as sluggish as hers right then.

"Do this," she ordered in a hoarse voice. Her throat had begun to constrict, and she doubted she'd be able to say much more.

She pressed her back against the seat and forced her legs upward into a tuck against her chest, gesturing for the others to do the same. Michael was the first to respond, and George after him. They crawled to the seat as quickly as their slowed reactions would allow, one on each side of Nancy. George grabbed Bess's arm and pulled her down also.

Nancy made a slight kicking motion at the partition in front of them to show what they were supposed to do. They'd need to kick together, but she could no longer speak so there'd be no countdown. She raised her arm as a signal. Her hand seemed to float through the air.

The rest of them had pulled their knees up and apparently understood that they were supposed to kick the partition together. Even Bess was in position. Their heels glanced off the Plexiglas out of sync in a random pattern.

Nancy's heart fell. It was their last chance. She looked at each of them in turn and in that glance she willed herself to convey the words she could not say.

Once more, she urged them silently. This is the one that counts.

She clamped her knees to her chest, staring at the partition through her tears, looking directly at the spot where her feet would hit—concentrating all of herself on that spot as if it contained the entire universe.

From somewhere deep inside her, out of a corner of herself she'd hardly known existed until that moment, came a surge of determination like nothing she'd ever felt before. It rocketed through her with a power she wouldn't have thought herself capable of.

"Now!" she shouted.

At that very instant, four pairs of legs shot forward in a single, mighty movement—hitting the partition and punching it forward to burst from its frame on Michael's side. He was out of his seat and pushing himself through the opening before Nancy had recovered from the jolting impact of the kick.

She could hear him fumbling with buttons in the front seat. With her last ounce of strength she reached over and grasped the door handle and pushed it down. It hardly budged at first, only clicked against the secure lock like the sound of doom.

Then the handle moved a few inches farther, and the door swung open with Nancy falling after it, tumbling into the cool night air—choking, sobbing, gulping her way back toward life.

Chapter

Ten

THEY ALL LAY on the ground near the limo and choked and gasped till they could breathe normally again.

Bess sat up and brushed weakly at an enormous grass stain on her dress. It had been made when Michael had dragged her away from the car. "My dress is ruined," she said with a shaky laugh.

They all could have made the same complaint. Evening outfits weren't made for scrambling around in life-or-death situations or kicking out partitions or sprawling on damp grass. Michael's white shirtfront wasn't gleaming any longer. In fact, it didn't even look white. Nancy's blue skirt had ripped when she had made that last desperate kick, and her stockings were a mass of runs.

"We're alive," croaked George. "That's what matters."

"They didn't mean us to be," said Michael. He'd been over at the limo, checking it out under the hood. "That car has been rigged with a switch on the dash to direct the exhaust back inside. They could have killed all of you just to get to me." He was holding on to his injured arm. He'd probably hurt it more pulling Bess from the car.

"I don't think they're only after you," said Nancy.

She told him about Kathy Novello's death. Michael's eyes widened as she retraced the scene in the copy room.

"So," Nancy concluded, "Kathy may have been killed because they thought she knew about you. But I'm not really sure how it all ties together."

"I swear I've never been anywhere near Kathy Novello's apartment building," Michael Mulraney said. "I didn't even know her."

"I believe you," said Nancy.

"Is all of this over that note I got about the real Mulraney?"

"Maybe somebody doesn't want us to dredge up the fact that he was probably murdered," George suggested.

"Could be," said Nancy.

"Franklin Turner couldn't have done all this," said George, gesturing toward the limo.

"If he did, he wasn't alone," said Nancy. "There was that other guy. The one with the deep voice."

"How would somebody like Turner be connected to the kind of people that probably killed Mulraney?" asked George, sounding confused.

"Only one person has the answer to that," said Nancy, standing up and brushing herself off. "I think I'll pay Turner a visit, but I don't think I'll be talking to him," said Nancy.

"But I thought you said you were going to visit him," Bess objected.

"I am." Nancy replied. "But, actually, I'm hoping he won't be home."

"Well, we're coming with you," Bess said. "It sounds too dangerous—" She stopped, overtaken by a fit of coughing.

"Bess, you're the greatest," Nancy said with an affectionate grin. "But you're obviously in no shape to do anything more right now. I'm sending you home to bed.

"You, too, Michael," she added, raising her hand to silence his protests. "You shouldn't have come out tonight in the first place. I want you to rest and recuperate."

"Well, *I'm* coming, no matter what you say," George insisted. Nancy gave her friend a grateful look. She'd hoped George would volunteer her help. Nancy's plan would require an extra pair of hands.

Meanwhile, Michael used the odds and ends from his pockets to disconnect the exhaust valve. The limo was still running, though the ignition key had been removed by the driver. Michael opened all the windows to air out the last of the gas and drove them back into town.

Nancy's Mustang and Michael's pickup were the only vehicles left in the parking lot of the Pinnacle Club. The reception was long over. Nancy wondered if there had really been a private supper for the councilman's "special friends."

Could Terry possibly be in on this? Could there be something from his past, something involving the real Michael Mulraney, that was a threat to Terry's career? He was clearly an ambitious man. How far would he go to protect those ambitions?

Nancy didn't mention her suspicions to George. She would be very upset that someone was looking for chinks in her white knight's armor, and Nancy didn't have the time or energy for an argument right then.

Michael took Bess home in his pickup, and George followed Nancy's car in the limo. The long car was part of Nancy's plan.

They parked out of sight from the entrance to the downtown luxury condominium complex. Nancy had driven by it that afternoon to check out where Turner lived. A doorman in a gray uniform sat at a desk just inside the double glass doors which led to the foyer. She and George would have to get past him to the elevators, and that wouldn't be easy.

"We have to distract him," Nancy said to George. "Phase one of Nancy Drew's master plan."

"Let's hope it works," George murmured. "Good luck!" She squeezed Nancy's hand.

The first stage of Nancy's plan involved using her messy appearance to her advantage. She rumpled her hair to look even worse before hurrying up to the building and through the glass doors.

"Somebody jumped into my car at the stoplight," she exclaimed. "I had to jump out to get away! Please—I need a phone."

She'd made that sound pretty convincing, but it was probably her torn stockings that actually convinced the doorman.

He was asking what he could do to help when the second stage of Nancy's plan got underway, right on schedule. George revved the motor of the limo after pulling it across the driveway entrance, just as Nancy had told her to do. The doorman looked toward the street and frowned at the long car. Then he glanced back at Nancy.

"You go ahead and take care of that. I'll wait here," she said with a smile.

The doorman looked toward the limo again. "I'll be right back," he said, and was off down the drive.

So far, so good, thought Nancy. Now all she had to worry about was whether George could make it up the drive without being seen.

A narrow sidewalk ran from the street to the building, bordered by waist-high shrubs. Nancy thought she saw a movement there, then George was out from behind the bushes and through the glass doors in a flash. Her athletic grace came in handy in tight spots like this one.

According to the directory board in the foyer, Turner lived on the fourteenth floor. George and Nancy took the elevator as far as the eleventh and walked the rest of the way, just in case the doorman had returned and was watching the floor indicator over the elevator door to see where they'd gone. It was quite late by now, and Turner's hallway was deserted.

"Are you going to pick the lock?" asked George as they stood in front of his door.

"First I'll see if he's home." Nancy pressed the buzzer. "I shouldn't really break in, but we're talking about murder here."

George had already darted out of view. "What are you going to do if he answers?"

"I'll think of something," said Nancy. She wished she felt as sure of that as she sounded.

There was no answer. Nancy had gambled on that, but the risk had been calculated. If Turner was as much of a party animal as George had said, then he probably wouldn't be home this early on a Friday night.

"That was easy," she said. "Now let's see if the easy way will work a second time."

She fished in her shoulder bag and pulled out a plastic credit card, which she inserted between the door and frame just above the lock. She slid the card down. It was the oldest trick in the book, but Nancy was banking on the fact that this was a doorman building in a well-patrolled, low-crime neighborhood. Maybe Turner hadn't bothered installing fancy locks. A barely audible click confirmed that he had not.

"This may still be our lucky night," said Nancy with a wink at George as the door swung open and they slipped inside.

She took out the flashlight she'd brought from the car and switched it on.

"Wow!" said George as the light beam bounced off expensive furniture and valuable-looking artwork.

"He couldn't possibly pay for this stuff on a political aide's salary, could he?" asked Nancy.

"I heard he doesn't get a regular salary," said George. "His parents pay him. That's how they got the councilman to take him on."

"Which just goes to show that maybe you *should* look a gift horse in the mouth," Nancy murmured with a grin.

Nancy moved away, scanning the walls for entrances to other rooms, then opening them to peer inside. At the third doorway she came across what she'd been looking for.

Books lined the shelves of what appeared to be Turner's study. The bindings looked suspiciously untouched. Nancy suspected Turner wasn't as much of a reader as he wanted people to think.

"The desk is over here," whispered George through the gloom.

Nancy was disappointed to find that none of the drawers was latched. Bad sign. People didn't keep secrets in open drawers, and she was looking for evidence that Turner had a very big secret indeed.

She searched the desk anyway, but she'd been right about locks and secrets. The deep drawer didn't even hold files, only a stack of thick phone books from around the country. Nancy pulled them out and stacked them on top of the desk as she examined each one.

She was about to put them back in the same order she'd found them when she was startled by something. The stack on the desk was noticeably shorter than the depth of the drawer. Yet, when she opened it, the top cover had barely cleared.

She tapped at the inside bottom of the drawer. It sounded hollow all right, and she could see it was inches above the actual base of the desk. She felt around inside.

"Maybe there's a hidden button or something like that to open it," George suggested, peering over Nancy's shoulder.

Nancy nodded, but she had, in fact, decided to try the easy way first. She pulled a nail file from her purse and fitted its thin blade along the side of the false bottom, then levered it upward.

They were in luck that night. Jackpot. Nancy lifted out a pile of manila file folders and leafed quickly through them. Sure enough, the name of Michael Mulraney was printed on one of the tabs.

She was about to open that folder and look inside when she heard the sound she had been dreading ever since they entered the apartment. A key was turning in the main door lock.

Franklin Turner was back!

Nancy took the three top files and stuffed them in her bag, then slid the false drawer bottom back into place and hastily replaced the phone books on top of it. She closed the desk drawer and listened. She could hear Turner moving around the apartment.

George had wedged herself into a corner next to the bookcase, but she wasn't really out of sight. Nancy flipped off the flashlight and crept into the kneehole under the desk. Their one hope was that Turner wouldn't have any reason to come into his study that late at night.

Then, the study door opened, and Nancy heard footsteps walking straight toward her.

It looked as if her lucky streak had run out.

Chapter

Eleven

THEY'D BE CAUGHT the minute he turned on the lamp. He'd see George for sure, and he'd have to step on Nancy to sit down at the desk. She held her breath and didn't make a sound. They'd have to run for it.

But he wasn't walking around the desk to sit down. He'd stopped on the other side. Instead of pressing the button for the desk lamp, he picked up the phone and pushed a button there.

Nancy had noticed the fancy telephone when she was searching the desk. It was the kind with the console that lit up when you lifted the receiver, and there was a row of buttons down the side for presetting numbers you called a lot. Turner must have pushed one of those just then and was waiting for it to ring and be answered.

The minute Turner spoke, Nancy knew her suspicion was right. Turner's was definitely the voice she'd overheard that first night from the copy room at Councilman Terry's office. It was squeaky from tension, just as it had been then.

"Franklin Turner here," he said nervously.

"Don't ask me," he continued after a pause to listen. "I have no idea how they got on to us."

He listened again. "I have no intention of backing out now. There's too much at stake."

Nancy couldn't tell if the person on the other end was urging Turner to back out or warning him not to.

"This girl and her friends were causing more trouble than they were worth."

He paused. "I'm doing my best and will continue to do so. You can be absolutely certain of that," he said, and listened one more time before hanging up without a goodbye.

Nancy was holding her breath, as she made a silent wish that he wouldn't turn the light on now. She could just see his shiny patent leather evening shoes as he stepped forward to search for something on the desk.

What if he looked for one of the missing file folders? She'd only taken three, hoping he wouldn't notice they were gone, but what if he did? Worse yet, she hadn't checked all of the desk drawers. Could there be a gun in one of them?

She was still imagining the unpleasant possibilities when the patent leather shoes turned aside and Turner walked back out of the study, closing the door behind him.

George let out a soft sigh of relief. Nancy unfolded herself from her hiding place and flexed the cramps from her legs. Still, she remained on guard, making a shushing sound in George's direction.

Nancy watched the crack under the study door till the line of light turned dark and she could hear no more movement in the rest of the apartment. Turner had probably gone into the bedroom.

Her eyes had grown accustomed to the dark. A slight shimmer of gray light came through the white drapes which covered the wide window behind the desk. She could make out the shape of the telephone console and reached for it.

The dial tone seemed very loud in the hushed room as she lifted the receiver. Just as she'd guessed, a light came on beneath the array of clear plastic buttons. She could see perfectly well to punch out a number if she wanted, but she didn't do that.

She was interested in the row of buttons down the right side of the console. Those would be the preset numbers. Turner had pressed one of them to make his call, but there were no labels to indicate what they were. And—this Nancy could barely believe—there was no Redial button. If only she could press one, she'd know instantly who Turner had called.

"What are you doing?" George whispered a little frantically as she crept from her corner. "Let's get out of here!"

"In a minute," Nancy whispered back as she pushed the top button in the preset row.

"Who are you calling?" George sounded even more frantic now. "There's a pay phone on the corner!"

Nancy raised a finger to her lips to silence George. Her face was eerily illuminated by the phone light.

A woman's voice answered on the other end of the phone line. "Yes," she said with a refined lift to her tone. Then she waited a moment. "This is the Turner residence," she added, unruffled as could be. "Celia Turner speaking. May I help you?"

Nancy pressed the receiver cradle to disconnect. That must have been Turner's mother. Nancy doubted that was who he'd been speaking to just now.

Nancy punched the next button. The wait for an answer was longer this time, and she heard the phone fumbled and nearly dropped on the other end before a young woman's voice responded with a sleepy "Hello."

Definitely not. Once again, Nancy pressed the cradle.

"What are you doing?" George repeated, more frantic than ever.

"Something important," Nancy whispered as she punched the third button. "I'll only be a couple of minutes longer."

She could feel George's agitation and hoped for a swift answer this time, but that wasn't what she got. The phone rang and rang, but no one picked it up. The same thing happened with the next two buttons. George grew more agitated by the second.

"Markson's Custom Tailoring," came the answer to the next call. "This is a recording. Please, leave your message at the beep."

The voice was even more refined than Mrs. Turner's had been, and with a definite British accent. Nancy smiled ruefully. From what she'd heard about Turner, she wasn't surprised that he thought it necessary to have his tailor on a preset button. She pressed the cradle and held it long enough to disconnect.

As she dialed again, George grabbed her arm. "I don't care how important this is. I want to get out of here right now!"

"Just one more, I promise." Nancy gently peeled George's grip from her arm. The fingers unclenched reluctantly, and Nancy pushed the remaining button.

Three rings followed by a click and a hum. Nancy could tell she'd come up with another recording.

"You've reached 555-8280," said a rather

bored female voice while music played in the background. "State your name, number, and the reason for your call."

As she'd done with Markson's tailoring shop, Nancy hung up before the beep. She silently repeated the number she'd heard to memorize it as she moved quietly away from the desk. She could see just clearly enough through the gloom to avoid falling over furniture as she tiptoed across the thick carpet with George in her wake.

Nancy listened at the door, then turned the knob ever so gently and eased it open. Like the dial tone, even the tiniest noise seemed magnified in the stillness of the apartment. Nancy forced herself to move slowly and carefully though her heart had begun to trip faster with each step. She'd pressed their luck by lingering so long. Now she was very much aware that they had to get out as fast as they could.

Nancy didn't breathe normally again until they were approaching her car. They'd made it out of the apartment, down the service stairs, and through a rear exit without incident. Then they hurried along alleys back to the street.

They kept close to the buildings and away from the streetlights as they scurried toward the car. They were almost there when Nancy pulled her friend abruptly into a doorway.

"Look," she said and gestured toward Turner's apartment complex, which was still visible from where they stood.

The doorman had acted fast. A tow truck had been backed around the semicircular driveway to get it into position in front of the limo. The tow chain stretched taut from the boom on the back of the truck to the bumper of the limo. A loud, metallic rasp shattered the night. George and Nancy watched as the front end of the long, black car was lifted from the ground and tilted steadily upward.

A few minutes later, the limo was angled high enough to be towed. The truck eased forward around the drive, then into the street with the big car suspended behind, only its rear wheels on the ground.

They drove right past the doorway where George and Nancy were hiding. As the truck moved off down the street, Nancy noticed a puff of exhaust smoke trailing from the limo's tailpipe. The big car was still running, its extra-large tank not yet out of gas.

"I wonder why they don't just drive the car away," George commented.

"Maybe it's not legal," said Nancy. "After all, it doesn't belong to them."

"It didn't belong to us, either, and I'm very glad to be rid of it," said George with a shudder.

Nancy didn't have to ask the reason for that shudder. "Why don't you stay at my house tonight?" Nancy asked when they reached the car.

George flashed the first smile Nancy had seen from her in hours.

"That sounds great!" she said, and the gloom lifted.

Nancy was up early the next morning. She crept quietly out of her room, leaving George breathing softly in the other twin bed. An hour later George went out on the wide front porch to find Nancy engrossed in the file folders on her lap.

She flipped the top file closed and gazed out across the peaceful, sycamore-lined street as if she didn't quite recognize where she was.

"There can't be any doubt about it now," she said, more to herself than to George. "Franklin Turner is definitely a blackmailer."

Chapter

Twelve

"WHAT'S IN THERE?" asked George, gesturing toward the folders.

"Sad stories," said Nancy, feeling pretty low herself.

"What do you mean?"

"Turner has information on these people about things from their pasts. Things that could cause them trouble now," Nancy explained.

"Like about Michael using someone else's name to get a job?"

Nancy nodded. "None of them are really big offenses, but these aren't big-name people. That's one of the reasons these revelations could be so devastating for them." She couldn't help feeling sorry for them. Although they'd done wrong, Turner's wrong seemed so much worse.

"How do you know Turner was blackmailing them?"

Nancy pulled a page from the top folder. "He made out one of these for each person. It lists the date a note was sent, then the amount asked for and the date it was paid. I'll bet there's a page like this in every one of those files back in his desk too."

George examined the paper. "This amount isn't that big. I thought blackmailers demanded hundreds of thousands."

"I've been thinking about that," said Nancy. "A blackmailer usually gets caught because he gets greedy. He asks for more than the victim can come up with, which sends the victim panicking to the police. Turner was too smart for that." Nancy felt nothing but disgust for his cleverness.

"He also asked for only one payment," she went on. "The blackmailer's second biggest mistake is that he keeps coming back for more until the victim feels like it will never end—"

"And panics and goes to the police," George finished. "Of course, there's no way to prove he wouldn't have gone back for additional payments."

"It doesn't look like it," said Nancy. "These entries begin a year ago, and he hasn't made return visits on any of them yet. But, of course, these are only three out of many." She heaved a sad sigh.

George looked thoughtful. "Do the victims have anything in common?" she asked.

"They all work for the city or were trying to work for the city when Turner went after them."

"I'll bet I know how he did it." George walked over to lean against the porch rail. She looked angry. "His starting this a year ago makes it obvious."

"What do you mean?"

"That's when Councilman Terry assigned Turner to work with the oversight committee." She came back over and sat down beside Nancy again. She still looked angry. "You see, he's good with computers. So he was given the job of checking out people whose names came up before the committee—"

"Because they wanted to work for the city, and the city doesn't want anyone who could bring scandal with them."

"Right."

Nancy shook her head in disgust. "They assigned the most corrupt person of all to find out who's corrupt, and he used the information to line his own pockets."

"I suppose you're right." George sounded discouraged.

"Remember what I said about looking gift horses in the mouth?"

"How could Councilman Terry have known Turner would do something like this?" George rose to her hero's defense.

"He should have run one of those computer checks on him," said Nancy, who was beginning to feel angry herself. "Criminals don't usually start their life of crime at Turner's age. I'd be willing to bet there's a string of petty offenses on his record going back to when he was in diapers."

"Unless he was always tricky enough to keep from getting caught." George looked more discouraged than ever.

"You've got a point," said Nancy.

"So what are you going to do?" asked George. "Take those files to the police?"

"Not just yet," replied Nancy. "Because of the way I got them, I'd like something to back them up in case they can't be used in court. I wish my dad were around so I could check it with him."

"So you need more proof. Do you have a plan?"

Nancy made a face. She really disliked this business. "I'm going to have to go see these people. If I'm lucky, maybe I'll be able to persuade one of them to come clean. But I don't think it's going to be very pleasant."

George looked at the name on the page Nancy had given her earlier. "Marjorie Rothman."

"She's first," said Nancy with a sigh.

"What did she do to get herself on Turner's hit list?"

"She made a mistake when she was very young. She borrowed from the accounts of the business she worked for. She paid back the

money, but she still got fired when they found out
what she'd been doing. She didn't put any of that
on her application to do property appraisals for
the city. If she had, it might even have been
overlooked."

"If it's such a small thing that she did, why
would she pay blackmail over it?"

"Guilt, I guess. She's probably very ashamed
of what she did and doesn't want anybody to
know. Maybe the amount Turner asked was small
enough to make it worth her while to pay and
avoid the trouble."

"She's going to have trouble now, isn't she?"
George sounded as solemn as Nancy looked.

Nancy stood up slowly. "Yes," she said. "She's
going to have trouble now."

Marjorie Rothman's house was small and neat.
Carefully tended shrubs bordered the brick path
to the stoop. The woman who answered the door
was also small and neat.

"May I help you?" she said in a friendly tone.

"Mrs. Rothman, my name is Nancy Drew. I'm
here to talk to you about Wyandot Realty," said
Nancy.

She'd gotten the name from the file, and men-
tioning it had exactly the effect she'd anticipated.
Mrs. Rothman's already petite form seemed to
shrink even smaller as she opened the door and
stood aside so Nancy could enter.

"Are you the one who sent that note?"

Marjorie Rothman asked after she'd sat down very primly on the edge of a chintz-covered sofa.

"No," said Nancy. "I'm not the person who blackmailed you, and I'm not here to threaten you now. But I am going to ask you to do something very brave."

"What is that?" asked Mrs. Rothman in a voice as small as she was. Her face was pale against her graying hair.

Nancy had come prepared to use pressure to get the information she needed. Instead, she spoke gently.

"I want you to help me to keep this man from doing the same thing to any more people."

"Was it a man? Do I know him?"

Nancy nodded yes to the first question. "But I don't think you know him."

"Have there been others like me—that he found out things about?"

"Quite a few."

Mrs. Rothman had been staring at the carpet ever since they sat down. "I'm not really very brave," she said, bringing her gaze to meet Nancy's at last. That look told Nancy that Marjorie Rothman was going to help in any way she could.

"My son, Bobby, was only three years old when my husband died," she began.

She told Nancy the whole story, about needing money desperately after her husband had died and left her with a small child to raise. She'd taken some money from the safe at her office in Chicago. She was going to pay it back, but the shortage was discovered before she could. She was fired, and to escape her shame she moved to River Heights. She never was in any trouble again.

Mrs. Rothman seemed relieved once she told her story. She told it even more willingly a second time, downtown for Chief McGinnis and Detective Hicks.

The police brought Franklin Turner in for questioning two hours later. When Chief McGinnis had heard Mrs. Rothman's story and seen the files Nancy had, he'd immediately applied for a search warrant. The minute it came through, he'd sent a team over to Turner's apartment. As soon as they had the evidence they needed, another team went to Councilman Terry's office and picked up their man.

The chief had consented to let Nancy observe the questioning from the next room through one-way glass.

Turner didn't appear to be the least bit upset by the arrest. He smiled arrogantly at the dark glass opposite him, as if he knew he was being watched and didn't care.

Nancy expected him to deny everything. After all, there weren't any witnesses. Mrs. Rothman had never actually seen him, and most likely his other victims hadn't either. He could hardly have missed his three top files between last night and this morning. And he didn't yet know that his home had been searched.

When the police chief strolled into the interrogation room with the rest of the file folders under his arm, though, Turner barely blinked an eye. Nancy was astonished at the way he admitted to the blackmail charges after almost no pressure at all.

"Almost everybody lies on résumés and job applications," he said with a cynical grin. "Some of those lies hide interesting stories. You just have to keep checking the dates and documents till you get to the truth. It's something like being a detective."

He turned his grin toward the mirror across from him. Nancy was certain he knew someone was there.

When asked about Kathy Novello, Turner showed his one and only glimmer of anxiety. "I wasn't there," he said in an agitated tone. Then he seemed to recover his confidence. "I wasn't there," he repeated, darting a smug look at the one-way mirror. "I was in a meeting the evening she was killed. You want witnesses? Ask Bradford Williams. Or Jethro Serkin. They were there too. We were discussing Tim Terry's campaign."

As for being in the copy room the night of Kathy's death, Turner swore he wasn't there either. Nancy hadn't dared tell the police all the details, since she didn't want to betray Michael

Mulraney's confidence. So they didn't question him about either of Michael's "accidents."

He supposedly didn't know anything about the tape in Nancy's car or the rigged limo either. He covered very well and didn't act surprised that she was still alive. "From what I've heard about Ms. Drew," he said, "I imagine she's made an enemy or two in her career."

That was his story, and he stuck to it, cool as could be, no matter how hard they tried to break him down. Nancy could tell that the police were inclined to believe him, but she had some questions they hadn't asked.

Why had he declined his legal right to have a lawyer with him while he was questioned, especially if he intended to confess to the blackmail? And why, since he was so good at stonewalling, did he confess at all? After all, he'd denied everything else.

Nancy put off her pondering when she heard Chief McGinnis ask why someone as well fixed financially as Turner would bother committing petty blackmail.

"Well, there's no such thing as *enough* money," he said with a smirk. "Besides, that nine-to-five stuff is a bore. I needed the stimulation of a challenge." The smirk broadened. "I wanted to see if I could do it."

Looking at his arrogant expression through the glass, Nancy realized that this was the only part of Turner's story that was the whole truth.

He was lying about most everything. She was sure that what he *wasn't* saying was what was really important to this very confusing case. But what was he hiding?

And could she find out in time to save Michael Mulraney?

Chapter

Thirteen

UNFORTUNATELY, CHIEF MCGINNIS didn't see things the way Nancy did.

"Of course we'll check his alibi. But it sounds airtight—and we have no evidence to link him to the Novello girl's death. There's no reason to believe he's not telling the truth," he told Nancy as they walked toward his office.

"You really believe her death was an accident or suicide?" she asked.

"Well," said the chief, "until we get some real proof to the contrary, I'm afraid we'll have to accept that explanation."

Nancy persisted.

"What about the limousine being sabotaged? And the tape in my car? Those weren't coincidences. He must have known about those incidents at least."

"Nancy"—the chief laid a fatherly hand on her shoulder—"I have a lot of respect for your talent. But Turner made one good point. You *have* solved quite a few cases in this town, and I think you have to look at the possibility that you may have made some enemies. We'll investigate, but I think it's more than likely the threats are not related." He gave her a tired smile.

"Right now, we've got a full confession from a blackmailer. He's out of commission, in jail. *If* we come up with anything that links him to these complaints of yours, I'll let you know."

Nancy looked at Chief McGinnis and sighed. "Thanks, Chief," she said, and did her best to smile.

Back at the small, neat house, by the time Nancy finished telling Marjorie Rothman about Turner's confession, the older woman's eyes had brightened considerably.

"All day long I've been afraid and relieved at the same time," she said. "It isn't easy to know that I'll always have to live with everybody knowing what I did." She blew her nose on the crumpled tissue she had been twisting between her fingers.

"I'm sorry I had to be the one to dredge all of this up," said Nancy.

She meant it. This was one "crime" she wished she hadn't uncovered.

"You mustn't feel that way, my dear," said

Mrs. Rothman. "For the first time in years I feel free. I can face life with a clear conscience. You've done me a great service."

"And I have to ask one of you." Nancy leaned forward and looked Mrs. Rothman in the eye. "I need your help."

"I'll do anything I can," said Mrs. Rothman. "What is it you need?" She seemed truly eager to help.

"I have a phone number I need to trace to an address. . . ."

"Of course. Since I'm an appraiser, I use all sorts of directories. It won't be any trouble—just follow me." Mrs. Rothman led Nancy to an immaculately organized study off the living room. She pulled a thick book with a green binding from a shelf over the desk.

"This is what you'll need. River Heights— Telephone Lines Indexed to Residence."

Nancy was relieved when Mrs. Rothman turned discreetly aside to look out the window. Nancy trusted the woman, but even so, people who knew too much seemed to find themselves in dangerous situations.

She scanned the listings and easily located the address corresponding to the phone number on the recording she had reached on Turner's phone.

"Thank you so much," Nancy said. She shook hands warmly as she said goodbye to Mrs. Rothman.

Maybe this phone number would turn out to

be a dead end, but it was all Nancy had to go on. She had to check it out as a last-ditch effort to uncover the truth.

Whatever that may be, Nancy added to herself as she hurried down the shrub-lined path to her car.

Looking at her watch, she was astonished to see that it was seven o'clock. It was too late to do any more today. Besides, she suddenly realized that she was starving. She hadn't eaten since breakfast!

Nancy stopped at a pay phone and called Hannah Gruen. "Where have you been?" the housekeeper asked, her voice full of concern. "Ned called twice. And Bess and George have been sitting here waiting for you to come back for the last hour. They almost had me convinced to call the police! What kind of case are you on, anyway?"

"Oh, Hannah." Nancy laughed. "I'm fine— except that I'm half dead of hunger. I'm on my way home now. I'll tell you all about it when I get there."

"All right," Hannah grumbled. "I'll scrape some dinner together. Just be glad your father's out of town, or we'd have search parties out by now."

"On my way," Nancy repeated, and hung up.

When she got home, she found that Hannah had "scraped together" roast chicken and potatoes, with blueberry pie for dessert. Bess and

George were only too happy to stay when Hannah pressed them, although Bess looked rather pale. "I haven't felt well since last night. A little carbon monoxide poisoning goes a long way toward killing an appetite," she said with a rueful grin.

"I have some news that should put you back on the road to recovery," Nancy promised.

Over the meal, Nancy brought them all up to date, sketching out the details of Turner's confession. She included a description, for George's benefit, of his obnoxious attitude.

"That creep. It makes me sick to think that someone so low could have ruined the lives of such good people," George said. Then she frowned. "Speaking of Turner's victims, I talked to Michael this morning. He's decided to go to the Immigration and Naturalization Service on Monday to turn himself in."

Bess gasped. "That means he's sure to be deported!"

"Yes, but his foreman will handle the business until Michael's brother can get here. The family has applied for and gotten immigration status. They've been on the list for three years, and Michael told me that their green cards came through."

Nancy understood how difficult it must be for Michael to take this step. His family would finally be coming to America, but he wouldn't be there.

"But it's not over yet," Nancy said. "Turner isn't the only one involved. Somehow his black-mail scheme has gotten him involved with Deep Voice. And Deep Voice is part of something bigger. And there's still Kathy's murderer."

"But isn't that Turner?" Bess asked.

"There's been no arrest," Nancy said, staring at her plate.

"I know the mystery isn't solved yet, Nancy, but do you think you'd have time tomorrow to come to a party for the campaign workers?" asked George.

"Sounds like fun. Where's it going to be?"

"Don't know yet. But Jethro Serkin is giving it."

Serkin! Nancy perked up. He was one of the people Turner had named for his alibi. She needed to talk to Jethro Serkin—and here was her chance. "Okay. I'll be there."

"Hey, Nan!" Bess piped up. "You'll never guess who called me this morning for details on last night's fund-raiser. Brenda Carlton! Do you think I should tell her about our adventure afterward?"

Nancy groaned. Brenda Carlton's father owned one of River Heights' biggest newspapers. But that fact didn't make Brenda a born journal-ist. She wasn't all that good at what she did, but she made up for it by being incredibly aggressive and obnoxious. She also liked to think of herself as a brilliant detective. More than once she had practically blown an important case for Nancy by interfering at the wrong time.

George was grinning. "I know, Bess. Why don't you send her to interview the man of the hour—Franklin Turner? I'm sure he'd have a lot to tell her. In fact, they might just get along really well."

Bess started to giggle. "Oh, George, don't give me any ideas!" she protested.

Nancy laughed too. Bess and George could always take her mind off her troubles.

She decided to forget about the case for the night. She'd take a hot shower, call Ned, get some sleep—and the next day she'd wrap the case up. The answers were all there, waiting for her to unravel. It was only a matter of time.

The next morning, as Nancy parked near the address she'd found in Marjorie Rothman's directory, she wished she'd enlisted her friends' help. She was in front of a downtown commercial high-rise, and she had no way of knowing which office belonged to the phone number from Turner's console.

Inside, she scanned the directory, recognizing some of River Heights' more prestigious law firms and private investment companies. Then she saw something she knew couldn't be a coincidence.

"Serkin, Edwards, Palmer, and Lang, Attorneys-at-Law, Suite 1500," read the listing halfway down the second column.

"Bingo," Nancy whispered.

The fifteenth floor was as deserted as the rest of the building. Someone had accidentally left the front door unlocked. But Nancy didn't doubt that there'd be pretty advanced security for the offices. She'd had some experience picking locks, but even her talents had their limits. A credit card won't do the job here, Nancy told herself, surveying the state-of-the-art office doors.

As it happened, she didn't need to be particularly resourceful after all. The door to Serkin's office was unlocked. Attorneys did work strange hours. Being the daughter of one had taught Nancy that.

She eased the door open and stepped quietly into a spacious reception area. There were no windows, but soft lights illuminated several eighteenth-century paintings on the walls. Plush maroon leather couches were placed at right angles to each other.

She was halfway across the thickly carpeted room when she heard voices. Whoever was working wasn't alone. She'd better do what she'd come for and get out fast.

She had to find out if the phone number from Turner's phone console corresponded to Jethro Serkin's office number. She had a strong suspicion that it did.

Crossing the room to the receptionist's desk, Nancy concentrated on making as little noise as possible. She tuned in to the hum of conversation coming from down the hall. If they heard her, they would stop talking, and that would be her signal to take off.

She leaned over to check the operator's phone bank, but before she could make out the number in the low light, she heard a rumbling bass voice behind her.

"Will this help?"

The desk light snapped on.

Chapter

Fourteen

THERE WAS NO MISTAKING that deep and threatening voice. It was the same one she had overheard in the copy room and again in the limousine.

"I don't believe we've been formally introduced," he said in a tone dripping with silky sarcasm. "I'm Jethro Serkin. By the way, can you see to find what you're snooping for? Could I make it easier for you by turning on more lights?"

Nancy looked down at the number on the phone. It was the same as the one from the recording she'd heard on Franklin Turner's phone. "I can see well enough," she said, trying desperately to keep the fear out of her voice.

"And now that you're here, Nancy Drew, you

might as well be comfortable." Serkin motioned to a tall, broadly built man standing in the doorway that led to an inner office.

"Do whatever it takes, Gus, to make sure she won't budge for a while. I'll be back." He turned to Nancy. "Then you and Gus and I will have a little chat."

Gus led her down a long hallway to a small office and tied her to a very uncomfortable Chippendale straight-back chair.

Nancy could hear Serkin's voice rumbling from the adjoining room. She could tell by the way his comments stopped and started that he was talking on the phone. She strained to hear, but all she could make out were his final words when he raised his voice to say, "Don't worry. She'll stay here."

Gus seemed amused. "Sometimes even the best detectives can find themselves in really tough spots. Looks like it's your turn."

Nancy knew she had to act quickly. Gus picked up a magazine and soon became engrossed. She tried to loosen the rope while he was preoccupied. But just as she was beginning to work the knot free, Serkin emerged from his office. He saw what was happening immediately.

"You idiot." Gus cowered under Serkin's withering stare. "First you lost Mulraney, then you botched the limo rig. Get the chloroform."

Nancy tried to struggle, but Serkin fixed her

with a look. "Don't even think about it," he advised. Then Gus returned and clamped a sweet-smelling cloth over her mouth and nose.

This is it, Nancy thought as she drifted away. My detective days are over.

"Nancy, wake up. Please."

Someone was yelling at her, but she was still too woozy to tell who it could be.

"Nancy. It's me. Michael Mulraney."

Images floated back across her brain. She thought she saw Gus's face. She forced her eyes to open, shaking her head to clear the cloudiness there. A dull throb pulsed at her temples as she remembered where she was. Then she saw Michael sitting across from her, tied to a matching Chippendale chair.

"I got a phone call saying you were in trouble," he explained. "I was to come alone and tell no one or else you'd be killed. That's what they said."

"Well, it's at least partly true. I am definitely in trouble. And now, Michael—"

Nancy didn't get the chance to finish her sentence. The door opened, and Jethro Serkin appeared.

"Did you sleep well? I certainly hope so, because we're all going to a party. And you, my friends, are the guests of honor. Though not, I'm afraid, for long."

Serkin grinned at Nancy and Michael as Gus

got them out of their chairs and shoved them along, still securely bound, out the door and up to the roof. There a helicopter was waiting, its rotor whirring in readiness for whatever journey Serkin had planned. "Where are we going?" asked Nancy.

"Don't worry. You're sure to enjoy yourselves. My friend's lakeside estate is a charming place to throw a lavish bash for hardworking campaign workers."

The pieces clicked together. Tim Terry's voter-registration-drive outing. It looked as if Nancy was going to be there after all. She leaned toward Michael and whispered what little she knew about the event. Serkin turned to look at them.

"You wouldn't be making plans, Nancy, would you?" asked Serkin. "You should be trying to guess what sort of surprise I have planned for you. Or are you too busy enjoying the scenery?"

Nancy had been looking out the window, trying to keep her bearings. They were flying away from River Heights, toward secluded Cedar Lake, where Ned Nickerson's parents kept a summer cottage.

If only Ned were there now!

After a short flight, they landed on a wide, manicured lawn. Serkin hadn't exaggerated about this being a lakeside estate. The house was large as a palace, and under other circumstances Nancy might have agreed that it was also charming.

Gus pushed Nancy and Michael from the helicopter, leading them across the expanse of lawn to a nearby enclosed veranda. Inside, the morning light and soft breeze played on the array of plants and flowers. Unfortunately, Nancy was in no mood to appreciate their beauty.

"What exactly do you have in mind?" she asked. "Why keep us in suspense?"

"You are about to meet a very important man, who also happens to be my boss." Serkin was enjoying his little guessing game.

He turned to greet a tall, distinguished-looking man dressed in tennis clothes who was strolling onto the veranda. He flashed a gold-toothed smile at her.

Nancy bit her lip. Suddenly she could hear Dee Shannon saying, "He never smiled . . ." It all made sense now. But why, oh why, had it taken her so long to figure it out?

When Nancy first saw him at the fund-raiser, Bradford Williams had impressed her as a pleasant, if bland-looking, man. Looking at him now she had a feeling she was going to have to reconsider that evaluation.

"Let me introduce myself, Ms. Drew," he said.

"Don't tell me—let me guess," Nancy said. "Michael Mulraney, I presume."

Williams's eyes flickered, and for a second Nancy had an ugly glimpse of his true character. Then he smiled, and the impression of charm and pleasantness returned. "Impressive!"

He turned to Michael. "My namesake. I'm so very pleased to meet you."

Serkin and Gus stood by as Williams took a seat in a white wicker armchair. As he talked, it felt to Nancy as if the airy and empty space around them had begun to fill with Williams's personality.

"It was a mistake to stir things up the way you have, Ms. Drew. You really should have left Mr. Mulraney—or perhaps I should call him Mr. Dougherty—to fend for himself. Why couldn't you simply back off when we asked you so nicely? Still, a man with my past has to admire such bravery."

Nancy remembered what she'd learned at the pool hall. She was dealing with a professional killer. "Your methods don't seem to have changed too much," she said. "Only now you have other people do the dirty work for you."

"Exactly. And Jethro tried very hard, on my orders, of course, to dispose of you. Usually he's quite good at that."

"But we managed to ruin your plans."

"Not just my plans. My future. Or potentially so. Until Franklin Turner's silly blackmail scheme uncovered the inconvenient presence of a second Michael Mulraney, I had succeeded masterfully with my little masquerade."

"You staged your 'death' very effectively," said Nancy, trying to give the impression she knew the whole story instead of only bits and pieces.

Williams smiled, his gold tooth glinting in the sun.

"Ah, yes. A little plastic surgery, a change of hairstyle, and a move to the big city go a long way," he said cheerfully.

"Why didn't you get your tooth fixed while you were at it?" Nancy asked, curious. "Do you know that people call you 'metal-mouth'?"

"Funny you should ask." Williams chuckled. "You see, this gold tooth has great sentimental value to me. I took my first hit job to make the money for this. I like to say my teeth were killing me."

Serkin roared with laughter. Nancy shuddered. These men were truly evil.

"Now, where were we?" Williams murmured.

Swallowing her fear, Nancy pressed on. "After a year or so you resurfaced and supposedly went into legitimate business. You obviously worked as hard at it as you did at your previous occupation."

"I had important people looking after things for me. It's easy to find that kind of help when you can afford it."

"People like the ones who spotted Franklin Turner when he got too close?" Nancy asked.

"Jethro was on to Franklin from the beginning. Activity in computer files shows up. It showed Franklin up."

"And now he's in jail."

"Franklin has been convinced there are advantages to his present position. He made a stupid mistake, leaving that copy in the machine. Realizing his stupidity, he stopped his petty blackmailing. Now he's realized how crucial it is that he not be stupid again."

"And Kathy Novello? Would you call her stupid also, Mr. Williams?" Keep him talking, she thought.

"You misjudge me if you think I caused that poor young woman's death." Williams leaned back and crossed his legs. "Kathy Novello was simply unlucky. She felt threatened, though Franklin was only trying to find out if she had the missing paper. She fled and apparently fell while running down the fire escape. It was an accident."

He said it so nicely, he almost made his excuses for causing a death sound reasonable.

"Franklin Turner is going to be taken care of," Serkin added. "We won't need to worry about him. Mr. Williams doesn't like loose ends."

Did that mean Franklin was going to be killed? If so, why had he volunteered that confession that Nancy now understood he'd made to protect Williams?

"Franklin will be so grateful to be alive he'll never think of repeating past mistakes." Williams answered Nancy's unspoken question. "And he'll be in Chicago where the exciting new job I have planned for him will quell his need for extracurricular activities as well as his need for funds."

"You're forgetting, Mr. Williams, that there's evidence against him," said Nancy, "and witnesses. Franklin Turner won't be in Chicago. He'll be in prison. Do you think your promises will be enough to keep his mouth shut there?"

"You are clever, Ms. Drew." He laughed. "But one must be crafty as well. That evidence you speak of will disappear. And as for the witnesses, there won't be any—not living witnesses anyway." His smile was more charming than ever.

"Especially not the two of you."

Chapter

Fifteen

How are you planning to dispose of us?" asked Nancy. Keeping up her cool façade was more of a struggle with every second.

"You've no doubt noticed how isolated we are here." Williams gestured toward the dense foliage just beyond the lawn. "I've always appreciated the peace and quiet, and sometimes it suits my business purposes as well. This is one of those times."

"My friends will know something is wrong when they can't get in touch with me." It was already past noon. She had been gone several hours. They were sure to suspect something was up when she wasn't ready for the party.

Williams frowned thoughtfully. "A dedicated worker like Ms. Fayne will attend the worker party. And when she and Ms. Marvin get here they'll understand why they haven't been able to find you this morning." Williams was smiling at his cleverness.

"Jethro has fueled up the cabin cruiser on the lake. When your friends arrive, they will hear that you and Michael went for a short ride. Unfortunately, you had a terrible accident."

This is too neat, Nancy thought. She searched for some way to convince Williams that his plan wouldn't succeed.

"Everyone knows I can handle a boat," she said. "They're sure to think it wasn't an accident."

"But, Nancy, you allowed Michael to pilot the boat. An error in judgment with a fatal result." Williams looked up at Serkin. "That's how it happened. Right?"

Serkin smiled. Gus chewed on a fingernail. Williams stared at her, as if challenging her to think her way out this time.

Michael's temper began to flare. Nancy could tell he'd been trying to keep it under control, but Williams's smug attitude was obviously too much to bear.

"You three will be prime suspects," he fumed. "There's no chance you'll get away with this."

Nancy took his lead. "My father is a very smart man, with friends in the police department. He's coming back to River Heights tonight, and this accident you're planning won't go uninvestigated."

"You must realize by now that I am beyond the reach of your father and his police friends." Williams laughed.

"Mr. Williams is an upstanding businessman," Serkin added. "No one would ever suspect him of any of this."

"Franklin's confession made sure of that," Williams added.

Nancy remembered Chief McGinnis's reluctance. Charging Turner had been enough for him. Without any evidence, McGinnis would see no reason to reopen the case.

Williams went on, "Besides, my day will be spent talking with Councilman Terry about campaign contributions. An airtight alibi, I would say."

With a veranda full of witnesses, Nancy thought. "You seem to have everything worked out," she said.

"Except for one thing," Michael said. "Now that Franklin Turner is in jail, Tim Terry will be watching his campaign for crooks like you. He'll be on guard."

"Terry is more naïve than you might think," said Williams. "Franklin showed us that about him. By the time the councilman realizes he has compromised himself, it will be too late."

Too late for what? Nancy thought. Suddenly

she saw the links that drew Serkin, Williams, and Turner's blackmailing victims together.

"Access to the oversight committee! That's what you're after!" said Nancy. "You want to control the councilman so your companies will get city contracts."

"You're quite the detective after all. River Heights will no doubt mourn your—disappearance."

Nancy glanced at Michael. Solving the mystery hadn't really solved anything. They were still in very serious trouble.

"It's quite simple," Williams concluded. "The real Michael Mulraney never got out of the construction business."

Williams smiled at his little joke, then signaled to Gus. "I think we've chatted long enough. Would you please take our guests down to the dock now?"

Serkin and Williams started down the veranda steps, talking between themselves as they walked away.

When they were halfway across the lawn, Nancy nodded at Michael. It was now or never. The two of them threw themselves at Gus, toppling him to the flagstones. The gun clattered from his hand and slid under a table.

Nancy delivered a deftly aimed kick to his right knee, and he howled in agony. When he tried to struggle to his feet, Michael smacked him down again.

"Good work. Now let's get out of here."

They headed for the opposite end of the veranda. There had to be another way out besides the one Williams and Serkin had taken.

They had obviously heard the commotion. Williams was running back toward the house. "Stop them!" he cried.

Serkin was already up the stairs ahead of him. Nancy and Michael had nearly made it across the veranda when Serkin grabbed Nancy from behind and motioned Michael to halt at gunpoint.

"That was very stupid," said Williams as he joined Serkin. "You take care of them, Jethro. Gus obviously can't get the job done, but I'm sure you can."

Nancy's skin crawled. She was sure he could too. As if to prove her right, Serkin took turns nudging her and Michael with the gun barrel all the way to the dock.

The cruiser was clearly a very rich man's boat, with its sleek modern look and solid teak interiors. Serkin gave them a tour.

"You might as well get a good look," he said as they walked along the starboard side. "After all, it's the last thing you'll ever see."

He pointed out that the cruiser could reach very high speeds. "You'll notice the modern technology here in the bridge. Automatic pilot. Sonar. Radar. Two engines in case one should fail."

How convenient, Nancy thought.

Serkin led them down into the cabin, which was lavishly furnished. There was even a leather sofa facing an entertainment center. Set into the ceiling of the cabin were little round bits of colored glass in a mosaic style reflecting the light above.

Throughout their tour, Nancy searched for a means of escape. She hadn't seen any tools or anything heavy enough to knock out Serkin.

He grabbed the two of them, pushing them into captain's chairs overlooking the boat's port side. "This is an expensive accident that you're going to have," he said as he tied them to the maple chair arms. "Everything on this boat is custom-made. Even these chairs have been designed to withstand high seas. That's why they're bolted to the floor."

Nancy had already noticed.

Serkin finished up by roping their legs to the rungs. "Have a wonderful trip," he said.

Nancy waited until he'd gone up the ladder to the bridge. "We've got to think fast," she said to Michael. "Any chance you're carrying anything sharp?"

"I already thought of that. Gus frisked me when I got to Serkin's office. There's nothing left."

The boat had begun to move. They were leaving shore, heading for a bend in the lake.

"We need to loosen these ropes." Nancy tried to will her heartbeat to slow down. "Move your legs back and forth slowly. Try to get some slack into the knots."

She and Michael struggled for several minutes. The cruiser suddenly took a sharp starboard turn, slowing slightly. Then Nancy heard another engine, less powerful than that of the cruiser, start up and move off into the distance.

The engines of the cruiser were roaring now, and they'd begun to pick up speed. The boat surged forward with a sudden jolt that threw Nancy back in her seat.

The same force had knocked Michael clean off his chair onto the floor. "Hey!" he yelled. His weight had broken the chair. That meant his arms were free. His hands were still tied in front of him, but not as tightly as they had been when the rope was stretched around the chair arms.

"Untie my legs," Nancy cried.

The cruiser was moving faster now, but all Nancy could do was watch while Michael picked at her knots with his tied hands.

At last he had untied her legs. "Hurry, Nancy. Don't wait for me," he gasped as he worked at his own bonds.

Nancy didn't bother answering. She flew out of the chair and stumbled to the ladder. She pulled herself up from rung to rung with her tied hands, then flung herself over the edge of the hatchway onto the bridge.

They were moving very fast now, at full throttle she would guess—breakneck speed straight ahead. She pushed herself up from the deck and stared across the bridge in disbelief.

There was no pilot at the wheel.

Chapter

Sixteen

THEY WERE ALREADY out of sight of Williams's estate, headed like a shot for the other end of the lake. And what lay at the other end was cliffs. Nancy knew that from her previous visits here, even if she hadn't been able to see those cliffs looming ahead each time the slamming prow of the racing cruiser dipped down.

It was obvious now what Williams had planned for them. Serkin had put the cruiser on autopilot—that must have been his dinghy's engine Nancy had heard earlier.

At this speed, the cruiser would come apart like a pile of matchsticks when it hit those rocks, and she and Michael would come apart with it.

Michael had stumbled up beside her and, between buffets of the bow smacking the water then bounding up again, he was pulling at the knots that still held Nancy's wrists.

"The throttle's jammed," she said when he had her free and she'd inspected the mechanism. "We have to get it back to a slower speed."

Her wrists burned where the ropes had been, but she didn't stop to rub them. They struggled with the throttle, but it wouldn't budge.

"Somebody rigged this as skillfully as they rigged that limo," Michael shouted over the roar of the powerful engines. "And look at the wheel!"

Nancy nodded as he pointed at the helm. She'd already seen the chain holding the steering mechanism on its course.

"What are we going to do?" shouted Michael, and Nancy could hear the beginnings of panic in his voice.

They didn't have much choice. "We'll have to swim for it," she shouted back as she headed for the rail.

"No!" he screamed, grabbing her arm. "I can't swim."

Now he tells me! Nancy thought, dismayed. She looked around for life preservers, but there were none. She didn't remember seeing any in the cabin either. Serkin had probably had them removed just in case she and Michael did get loose.

"I'll tow you," she said.

"That won't work."

He was yelling at her, and she could tell that it

wasn't just because of the noise of the engines. He was near full panic now. She had to calm him down.

"I'm a strong swimmer," she shouted. "We'll make it."

She was doing her best to sound reassuring, though she had her doubts that she could actually get them both through the treacherous current to safety.

"I'm telling you it won't work," he insisted. "I lose my head in the water. I'll pull us both down."

Michael's brogue was so thick now that she would have had trouble understanding him even in quieter surroundings. Still, she knew one thing: A panicked person could be deadly in the water. She could knock him out and tow him, but she wasn't sure that would work in this current.

She glanced through the spray-spattered windshield at the rapidly approaching shoreline. Clouds retreated over the looming cliffs. *I will get us out!* she told herself.

"Let's check the engine," she shouted. "Maybe we can stall it somehow."

Serkin had pointed out the engine room during his tour. The door was locked, of course. But Michael flew at it with a force she wouldn't have thought possible for a man of his size.

On his third run, the door splintered and fell backward in response.

Inside, the heat was nearly overpowering.

Steam pulsed from huge pistons, and the roar was deafening. There was no way they could talk to each other in there, not even at shouting volume. Suddenly Michael had Nancy by the arm and was pulling her back outside and toward the bridge deck once more.

"What are you doing?" she protested, but he was hauling her along too forcefully for her to slow their progress much.

"I know a little bit about engines," he shouted once they were far enough from the engine room that she could understand what he was saying. "We couldn't so much as lay a hand on those machines now. They're too hot. They'd sear our skin off in a second. And there weren't any tools around to use either."

Nancy saw immediately the truth of what he was saying and stopped trying to resist as they stumbled up onto the bridge.

"Besides, there are two of them," he went on. "Even if we could shut one engine down, there's no way we could disable *two* in time to keep from hitting those rocks."

The cliffs were closer now. Nancy knew Michael was right.

"We have to think of something else," she hollered, trying not to sound as bereft of hope as she suddenly felt.

"There's no other way," said Michael, looking resigned to his fate. "We have to jump."

"Maybe we can find something that will float," Nancy shouted. "Something less obvious than a life preserver."

Michael looked skeptical, but she'd already pulled herself free of his grasp and was stumbling toward the cabin.

"Check the port side," she shouted. Seeing his confusion, she added, "Around to the left," and pointed at the opposite rail.

He nodded and weaved away.

They were running out of time, and Nancy knew it. A few minutes more and they'd have to jump for it no matter what the risk to either of them. She stared through the hatchway into the cabin, trying desperately to think of a way out of this.

Then she saw it. Why hadn't she thought of that before? She was down the ladder in a flash, falling on the last step and picking herself up, hardly even noticing she'd fallen.

She stumbled to the bench that ran along the cabin wall and began pulling at one of the cushions. Fancy boats were most often furnished with flotation cushions. She hoped with all her heart that this cruiser was no exception.

The ties that held the cushion tore loose, and she staggered toward the ladder with her cumbersome burden. The cushion would lose its awkwardness in the water—unless it wasn't a flotation device at all. In that case, it would waterlog very fast and sink like a boulder. Nancy tried not to think of what would happen if Michael was clutching it at the time.

He had finished his circuit of the portside deck and was back at the hatchway as she emerged and handed the cushion up to him.

"We have to hurry!" she shouted. The cliffs were really close now. "If we're lucky this cushion will float. Then you just hold on tight to it, and we'll get you to shore."

They were at the rail now. She saw the fear flicker in Michael's eyes. Then it was gone, and she knew he was going to jump without further question when she told him to. She admired him so much for that she would have hugged him if there'd been time. Instead, she climbed onto the rail and motioned for him to do the same.

"Jump as far from the boat as you can. Whatever you do, don't freeze up. We're going to make it."

He pulled himself up next to her.

"Wait for my signal," she shouted.

Nancy paused a moment, feeling for the rhythm of the up-and-down movement of the prow as it plowed through the waves. They had to jump when the bow was as high as possible out of the water. That would give them more of an arc to get clear of the boat's churning wake.

A few more seconds—now!

"Jump!" she cried.

The cold September water struck her with a jolting shock. She swallowed water and spray as she was forced beneath the surface by the momentum of her leap. She'd grabbed Michael's arm so they would jump together, but her hold slipped when they hit the water. As she fought her way to the surface, she had no idea whether she would find him there or not.

She broke through into the sunlight and shook the water from her eyes. There he was, about ten feet away. He was holding tight to the cushion, and, sure enough, it was supporting him. Unfortunately, he was still in the cruiser's wake, though Nancy had thrown herself clear. She propelled herself toward him, stroking overarm.

The boat was past them now, roaring off toward the cliffs. Meanwhile, a surge of wave, created by the cruiser's rampage through the water, was headed straight at Nancy and Michael. She grabbed him and stroked one-arm with all her might till she could feel that they were free of the wake. Still, she kept stroking hard as she could.

"Kick!" she hollered at Michael as her own legs whipped up and down beneath the surface.

It wasn't the current she was so intent on escaping now. She didn't look up to see. She didn't have to. She could hear what she'd been dreading. In fact, she was sure everyone for miles must be hearing it too, as the cruiser hit the cliffs with a crash of metal and shattering glass.

Nancy kicked harder still. Maybe two seconds passed, though it seemed much longer.

Then the most dreaded sound of all assaulted the autumn afternoon, as what was left of the cruiser exploded in a gush of flame.

Chapter

Seventeen

A CHUNK OF FLAMING DEBRIS hissed into the water barely two yards away. Nancy waited for the sizzling to stop before reaching for the piece of wreckage as it floated past. She doused it thoroughly to cool it off. Unlike the cushion, this piece of wood was big enough for two.

"Grab on to this with me," she told Michael. "Then let go of the cushion."

Michael had been clinging so tightly to the square of foam and fabric that it took him a moment to give it up. When he had hold of the wreckage at last, he and Nancy began to kick.

The current was strong, but with the floating debris to buoy them up and both of them working together, they would make it to the shore.

By the time Nancy and Michael dragged themselves out of the water and back along the shore to Williams's mansion, the campaign-workers' party was in full swing. The band had set up and was playing rock and roll much too loudly for anyone to have heard the cruiser explode.

The lawn and garden were filled with people. A pleasant breeze fluttered the flowered cloths on the long tables. They were set with dishes that looked far too elegant, in Nancy's opinion, for eating on the lawn.

A chef in a tall, white hat supervised the barbecue area like a captain of a ship. Several cooks of obviously lesser status, wearing much smaller hats, scurried about with heaping platters of smoked turkey, ribs, and chicken to add to those already brimming with corn and salads and baskets of rolls.

From behind some shrubbery, Nancy noticed Jethro Serkin a few tables away. He'd come up to Bradford Williams, who was deep in conversation with Councilman Terry. Serkin appeared to be pretty upset. He pulled Williams aside and whispered something in his ear.

"I wonder what's going on over there," Nancy whispered to Michael.

"It looks like some kind of high-level discussion," he said.

The expression of sudden sorrow on Bradford Williams's face would have convinced anyone but Nancy that he'd just had a terrible shock.

"They're pretending they've just heard about us!" she whispered as the realization hit her.

Then she spotted George and Bess emerging from the crowd. Nancy had a strong suspicion what Williams was intending to say to them. Meanwhile, he couldn't have looked more solemn as he laid a protective hand on George's arm and eased the overflowing plate of food from Bess's hand.

"I think we should go inside," he said in a gentle tone as Nancy moved out of the bushes and close enough to hear. "There's something I have to tell you."

"What's going on?" said George, her eyes widening.

"It would be better if we talked about this privately," said Williams.

"I disagree," said Nancy, stepping out from behind a nearby clutch of partiers. "I think you should say what you have to say right here where everyone can hear. I think they'd all be interested in sharing your sad news, Mr. Williams. Or should I call you Mr. Mulraney?"

George's jaw dropped. "Nancy! What happened to you?" she exclaimed.

"Tell them what's going on," said Nancy, who had not taken her eyes off Williams.

She noticed him falter a moment, almost imperceptibly. Then he composed himself again. He nodded at Serkin, who stepped toward them, slipping his hand inside his jacket.

"Look out. He's got a gun!" shouted Michael as he ran up behind Serkin.

The crowd turned to stare as Michael wrestled Serkin to the ground. Williams took advantage of the distraction and headed across the garden.

"Stop him!" Nancy cried. "Don't let him get away!"

She raced after Williams, shoving some of River Heights' more prominent citizens out of her way as she ran. The bewildered guests obviously had no idea what to do.

By the time Nancy broke free of the crowd, Williams was through the garden and out of sight. Nancy guessed he was heading for his helicopter launch pad. She cut through some shrubbery, ignoring the branches that caught at her soggy clothes. She wasn't about to let him get away now!

As she emerged onto the lawn, she spotted Williams. He was almost to the copter, and he was signaling the pilot to start the engine.

"Nancy, what's going on?" cried George, whose long strides had finally closed the gap between her and Nancy.

"We can't let Williams take off," Nancy shouted over her shoulder. "Call your volunteers!"

George immediately stopped in her tracks. Putting her fingers to her lips, she gave a piercing whistle. "Everybody! Over here!" she screamed.

146

In a moment a fast-growing crowd was running across the lawn toward the helicopter pad.

Williams had climbed into the helicopter by the time Nancy and her troops reached the launch pad, but he hadn't yet closed the door behind him.

"Grab onto the runner," Nancy shouted as she caught hold of Williams's arm. "This man is a killer—we can't let him get away!"

The youthful volunteers, who had done such a wonderful job of getting potential River Heights voters to register, rose to the challenge once again. They pounced on the nearest of the copter's two runners, pulling the big bird off balance just as it had begun to rise from the ground.

Nancy nearly lost her grip on Williams as the copter tipped and weaved.

"Pull harder on that runner," she urged the still-growing ranks.

More volunteers had arrived and leapt into action.

"Get us out of here, you fool," screamed Williams at the pilot.

The pilot struggled with the controls as George joined Nancy in tugging at Williams's arm.

"He's going for a gun," shouted George as Williams reached for a compartment between the seats.

But before he could latch onto a weapon or anything else, George and Nancy had pulled him

147

from the cockpit. He came out headfirst, nearly taking Nancy with him as he fell. Then he was on the ground with George on top of him and a number of her volunteers following suit.

Nancy heaved a sigh of relief. The real Michael Mulraney had been caught at last.

Two days later Nancy, Bess, and the other "Michael" were at the councilman's office helping George pack up her materials from the voter-registration drive.

"It looks like Tim Terry isn't going to make it to Washington after all," said George mournfully. "In fact, I doubt he'll even be a city councilman after the next election."

"Not when this oversight committee scandal hits the newsstands," said Bess.

Brenda Carlton had already been around asking questions for an article for her father's paper.

"Hiring that creep Turner was a big mistake," Bess went on. "It looks like Mr. Terry is going to pay for it with his career."

"Bess!" Nancy warned.

Michael put his arm around Bess's shoulders and took a more diplomatic tone. "I don't think George wants to talk about the councilman's future right now."

"That's okay," said George. "I can take it. Besides, who knows what Tim Terry's future will be? He's a smart man and a shrewd politician.

He may come out of this better than we think. I do know one thing though."

"What's that?" Nancy asked.

"Whatever happens to him, I'm one person he won't have on his team." George fitted the last stack of flyers into the box she was packing. "My public service is going to be confined to the voter-registration drive from now on. I can be sure that's a good cause."

"My father is glad you took him up on his offer to work out of his office," said Nancy.

"I'm really grateful to him for that," said George. "It means the drive can go on without a hitch." She grinned mischievously. "And now that Bess has some free time, I know she's dying to help."

Bess looked resigned. "Yeah, well, Jeff was cute, but his sole interest in life was being the Video King." Suddenly she brightened. "Hey, isn't this the recruiting season for young lawyers?"

Nancy and George laughed. "I think you finally figured out how to get Bess to do her civic duty," Nancy joked, poking George in the ribs.

Michael lifted the last box onto the hand truck they'd borrowed from the Municipal Building maintenance department.

"I feel like I owe Mr. Drew even more thanks than George does," he said.

"My dad is only too happy to negotiate with

the immigration office for you," said Nancy. She grinned. "Especially since you said you'd speak at the voter-registration rallies. He's very interested in your case. He thinks he may even be able to convince the INS to let you stay in the States."

"Speaking at those rallies is the least I can do. And nobody knows better than I do how much it means to be a citizen of this country, because nobody ever cared more about getting to be one."

"When is your family coming?" Bess interrupted. "I can't wait to meet your brother."

They all laughed.

"That's our Bess," said George.

"It will take a month or so for Jamie and the rest of the Doughertys to make it through the red tape to River Heights," said Nancy. "In the meantime, this is so we won't forget who our first future citizen really is."

She pulled a name tag from her pocket and pinned it on Michael's shirt. She'd found it in a box of supplies left over from the fund-raiser and had written a name on it in big letters that were bright, Irish green.

He looked down at the tag and read aloud with a bit of a brogue and a catch in his voice:

"'Hello. My name is Kevin Dougherty.'"

Nancy's next case:

Superstar Jesse Slade has been missing for three years—until Nancy spots a clue on the videotape of Slade's last concert. She and her friends George and Bess fly to California to find out what really happened to the rock singer.

The first bombshell is that Slade's manager, Tommy Road, vanished at the same time. Posing as a VJ at a rock TV station, Nancy digs deeper into the music scene. Riches and fame are tempting prizes, but can they lead to murder? Nancy uncovers the answer in a deadly sound studio that pumps out killer music. All oldies but baddies . . . in *VANISHING ACT,* Case #34 in The Nancy Drew Files™.

A NANCY DREW & HARDY BOYS
SUPERMYSTERY™

Shock Waves
By Carolyn Keene

Nancy Drew and the Hardy Boys team up for more mystery, more thrills, and more excitement than ever before in their latest Super-Mystery!

It's Spring Break, and Nancy, Bess, George, and Ned meet Frank and Joe Hardy on sun-drenched Padre Island, Texas, in order to do some scuba diving. The excitement builds when Frank and Joe's friend buck sees a dead body underwarter. Soon, thefts begin to disturb the island's residents. When Buck's life is threatened and Nancy's friend Mercedes is kidnapped, it becomes obvious that someone wants Nancy and the Hardys to stop their investigation, and fast! Nothing can stop Nancy and the Hardys though, and the thrilling climax of Shock Waves will have you in shock!

COMING IN APRIL 1989